Stand Alone Novel

ALSO BY LOU WILHAM

The Curse of The Black Cat

Tales of the Sea Witch
A SEA WITCH ORIGIN STORY

LOU WILHAM

Copyright © 2020 by Lou Wilham

All rights reserved.

No part of this book may be reproduced in any form or by any electronic or mechanical means, including information storage and retrieval systems, without written permission from the author, except for the use of brief quotations in a book review.

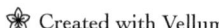 Created with Vellum

*For Lissa & Val,
who gave me the courage to
build worlds from words.*

Tales of the Sea Witch
A SEA WITCH ORIGIN STORY

Prologue

From the lowliest of sea urchins to the most powerful of witches, everything under the sea is born and must die before it can be born again.

In between birth and death, each creature lives with at least a drop of magic in their veins. This magic connects one being to another, joining two halves of a whole—a soulmate is what the merfolk call it. A creature could live for centuries, never having found their other half, but when they have joined it makes each more powerful for the connection. Should they lose that other half, the magic in their veins can sour and twist into something that can only be described as dark.

No creature is born dark; they have darkness thrust upon them. Such is the case for the infamous sea witch. Her name—lost long ago to the vagueness and obscurity of being labeled a villain—but for our purposes, we will call her Irsa.

Chapter One

Born to a doting mother and a frequently absent father, the gray-haired child arrived as most merbabes do in a flurry of bubbles and wailing. Her father — a merchant named Calix of some small fortune — was not so mysteriously absent on the day of her birth.

"Where do you suppose he is?" Irsa's grandmother — a graying, bent battle-ax of a merwoman named Diantha — growled, glancing out the window at the darkening ocean once more.

"He's busy, Mother, don't you fret. We got through just fine, didn't we little Irsa?" Hali asked, bending her head to brush a kiss to the child's head. Innocent black eyes peered up at her from her arms, the child making a soft, satisfied noise at the attention.

"Irsa? Tck," Diantha muttered in disgust. When Hali paid her no mind, the old woman continued, "Couldn't you have chosen something more normal? I thought you would name your firstborn after your father — Poseidon rest his soul — Dorian."

"No," Hali responded primly, sinking back further into

the soft bed of kelp beneath her. Her fingers brushed along the delicate amethyst scales of the baby's little tail. Irsa murmured affectionately up at her mother before promptly drifting off to sleep in her arms.

"What an odd-looking child," Hali heard her mother mutter before she twirled to watch for Calix, again.

Hali's nearest and dearest friend Evadne gave birth to a fire-haired little girl whom she named Aislin, not but a fortnight later.

Hali laid Irsa next to the bright-haired baby in the kelp lined crib and laughed softly. "How strange they look," she murmured mostly to herself.

"Hm?" Evadne asked. She swam over to peer at the infants lying side by side in the crib.

Hali looked up, shaking her head ruefully. "I was just thinking — they seem to complement each other so nicely."

Indeed, the pair was quite the sight laying side by side as they were. Aislin's shimmering jade tail flapped, and the baby began to fuss. Then Irsa's amethyst tail reached out to press one gauzy fin to the other child's, and her chubby hand wrapped around Aislin's, and like that the two merbabes were silent once more.

"They will be the best of friends," Evadne announced with pleasure.

"Yes, they shall," Hali agreed, hugging the other woman tightly and laughing with her.

And they were the very best friends the tiny village of

Tjena ever saw. From that moment onward, Aislin and Irsa were inseparable.

"The first one to the bookshop gets to pick the story," Aislin shouted over her shoulder with a giggle as she raced down the street, her shimmering tail whipping along behind her creating a stream of angry bubbles.

"That's not fair! You got a head start!" Irsa shrieked back, but she was laughing. She squeezed her dark eyes shut, the water rushing through her hair. In her hurry to keep up with Aislin, she bumped a merman with his arms full with baskets of crabs, clicking their claws together in agitation.

"Hey! Look where you're going, little girl!" The blond hunter growled, throwing up a fist to shake it at her — nearly dumping his catch to the sand.

Irsa whipped around him with some trouble, still laughing. "Sorry!" She called over her shoulder before turning back to continue her mad dash to beat Aislin to the bookshop.

"I win," Her freckled friend declared triumphantly, panting hard from their race. "Which means we're reading a princess story!"

Irsa rolled her eyes scoffing. "You always want to read about princesses. They're so boring." She complained. "Can't we read about something exciting for once? Like pirates!"

Aislin shrugged, her face still lit with a broad smile that made her green eyes shine. "Maybe next week. Come on, Irsa, don't be a guppy about it." The little girl spun, her long red hair sweeping out around her, and then headed into the shop without another word.

"I'm not a guppy," Irsa muttered irritably.

An hour later found the two little girls laid out on the soft sand of the small shop, a book of fairytales open before them. Irsa yawned in boredom, as Aislin read aloud. "And then he went down on bent fin and proposed. And they lived happily ever after," Aislin exhaled dreamily. "Isn't that romantic?"

"Yeah, sure, romantic," Irsa grumbled, rolling over onto her back to stare up at the carved coral ceiling.

Her friend glanced at her, a frown tugging down the corners of her lips. "What's the matter?" When Irsa didn't answer, Aislin gave her a soft nudge with her fin. "This isn't about the trials, is it?"

Irsa shrugged, not wanting to voice her concerns. She felt silly for being so worried. It was inevitable, and beyond her control. They would be tried, and then their lives would be decided for them. That was the end of that.

"Irsa—talk to me," Aislin insisted softly, unable to stand the worried expression that creased her friend's brow. She reached over with her fingers to smooth the wrinkle in Irsa's forehead.

The other girl didn't it away, but she didn't meet Aislin's eyes either. "It's just…" Her words drifted off for a moment in embarrassment. "What if I don't have any magic at all? What if I'm to be a-a-a sand cleaner?" She stuttered the words in mortification. "Princesses don't talk to sand cleaners." A bark of laughter left Aislin, drawing Irsa's dark eyes to her. "What?"

"You're much too smart to be a sand cleaner," Aislin said between chortles. "If anyone is destined to scavenge the sand for land debris, it's me. Stop being silly."

Irsa huffed, an irritated bubble floating up above her. "You and I both know it's not about smarts! It's how much magic you have. And if I have none, they'll apprentice me to someone boring."

The fire-haired mergirl's giggles died down, and she shook her head. "Even if they do, you'll think your way out of it." She tapped Irsa's forehead gently, grinning down at her. "Trust me, you've got nothing to worry about."

Then she took one of Irsa's hands in hers and gave it a firm squeeze. The simple gesture soothed Irsa's worries, and in a moment the pair were back to normal. All thoughts of the trials wiped away by childish chatter of princes and far-off waters.

Chapter Two

Soon, the trials were upon them. Aislin's was in the morning, Irsa's that evening.

The carriage swayed in the water, tugged along by two brilliantly colored seahorses, but Irsa could not appreciate the journey. Without Aislin to keep her mind from wandering, Irsa imagined all manner of tragedies awaited her in the open ocean.

Hali reached out to take her daughter's chubby hand in her own to soothe her. "You'll do just fine," she whispered.

The carriage ceased its swaying, pulling to a stop before a collection of ocean smoothed rocks. The rocks themselves were nothing special—Irsa had seen such rocks many times. What was unusual was the formation they were in, each stone propped precariously on its smallest side, one beside the other in the shape of a circle. A young boy—tasked with driving the carriage—came to open the door for her. "Thank you," Irsa whispered, stalling in the door to stare down at the clean white sand beneath her.

"Ma'am?" The boy asked, swaying awkwardly in the water.

"Go on Irsa," Hali nudged her lightly with the tip of her fin.

Irsa nodded and swam out towards the rocks, wincing when the carriage door shut behind her. Gulping, the mergirl made her way to the small opening between the rocks where a guard waited for her. "Irsa—daughter of Calix and Hali of the village of Tjena?" His voice boomed in question, reading her name from a list in his hand.

She nodded her head to acknowledge that was who she was. He lifted his arm to usher her inside, his muscles shifting beneath a well-cut tunic emblazoned with the royal seal. Inside the tightly packed rocks were three sea witches waited. As Irsa swam closer, three pairs of eyes narrowed on her with interest.

"Come here, child," one of them said. She extended her elegant hand to Irsa, shimmering golden eyes fixed on the girl with an intensity that caused Irsa's stomach to twist uncomfortably. In her discomfort, her fin refused to move her forward, frozen to the spot. "Tsk," the witch murmured. "I said come here, child," she repeated with a growl, this time her magic flowed out of her in glittering waves of gold. It wrapped around Irsa's tiny form and yanked her closer.

Irsa yelped, her tail flapping to escape, but the magic refused to relinquish its hold. "Let go of me! Leave me alone," she cried. With much squirming, it deposited her before the three witches, who circled her quickly, leaving her no means of escape.

"Give me your finger," a merman with thin lips and hair the color of rotting kelp growled. It was as if the words compelled her. Irsa had no choice, she held out her finger to the man. From somewhere within his long flowing robes, he pulled a knife.

Irsa squeezed her dark eyes shut, but that didn't help her escape the pain as he pressed the tip into her finger to draw blood. She whimpered loudly, yanking her hand back when she was free of his compulsion. Through the thin layer of her lids, Irsa could see the flashing of lights. When she opened them, she found that the stringy blood glowed violently with a pale purple light. "Wh-what?" She asked, confused.

A soft murmur left the witches as they eyed the shining blood with interest, seeming to have forgotten the child it had come from. Above the pounding of her heart in her ears, Irsa struggled to make them out. Words like powerful and strong only just reached her hazy mind.

"Is the young miss finished?" The guard asked, not daring to enter. "Her mother is looking mighty antsy."

"Nearly," the female sea-witch responded. Then she reached her elegant hand to rest atop Irsa's gray head. A soft murmur of words unknown to the child floated through the air. Blinding magic left Irsa blinking back tears. A moment later, she exited the rocks holding her still throbbing finger.

The guard guided her back to the carriage, helping her up inside once more where her mother waited with open arms. "Wh-what happened," Irsa asked.

"I don't know darling, but you're safe now," Hali murmured, pressing a kiss to her daughter's head. "I'm here now."

"Why can't I remember?"

"That's how it is meant to be. We'll know the results soon enough, and we have a long drive back to Tjena. Try to rest." Hali's voice was soft and soothing to the little girl. Her tender hands stroking Irsa's back as she curled up in her mother's lap and soon drifted off to sleep.

She slept on for a time, the stress and trauma of the trial having worn her out. When the first jolt of the carriage came, Irsa didn't wake. It was the third that finally roused the sleeping child, her dark eyes wide with fear. "Mama, what's going on?" She asked, scrubbing at her eyes.

"Get out of the way, boy," a man growled from just outside the carriage door—fury so clear in the tone it sent a shiver down Irsa's spine. What followed was a muffled thud, a yelp, then the door was ripped from its hinges in a flurry of bubbles. On the other side floated a man with violent amber eyes, a bandana covering the bottom half of his face. Irsa had but a moment to register what was happening—bandits—and then the man grabbed her mother's arm and ripped Hali from the carriage.

"Mama!" Irsa lurched forward to grab at her mother's other hand, but it was too late. The man slung Hali down on the sand, holding a knife dangerously in her direction. "Leave her alone!"

"Shut up girl," he growled from behind his bandana, his eyes not leaving Hali. Irsa swam at him, full speed, with no real plan. A second later, her ears rang with the force of his backhanded smack. She too crumpled to the sand with a whimper. Irsa lost track of things, unable to understand what was going on.

"Irsa!" Hali shouted, pushing onto her hands to swim to her child.

The man stopped her, holding the knife threateningly again at her. "Your money and jewels," he ordered tossing a half-full sack onto the sand beside her. "Put it in the bag, and no one gets hurt."

"I-I have nothing like that," Hali whispered.

"Put it in the bag, Hali." He bent over her, pressing the knife closer to her belly. "Or I'll gut you and leave you out here to die."

Hali's eyes widened in recognition. "Argus?" She gasped.

It was then that Irsa came back to consciousness, in

time to see the tip of the blade sink into her mother's bare belly. A high-pitched screaming permeated the surrounding water—it took Irsa too long to realize it was her. Blood flittered around them, and the man bent to pluck Hali's purse from her side. "You should have kept your mouth shut Hali," he growled.

Bubbles flittered around him as he spun to grab a seahorse and make his escape. The tiny mergirl floated in his way. Irsa's black eyes glowed silver and amethyst power slithered out around her like tentacles. "You're not leaving." Her voice echoed on the current.

"Get out of the way, girl," Argus snarled, his amber eyes flashing dangerously.

"No." Before he could swipe his knife towards her, a tendril of magic smacked the weapon from his hand. Then another wrapped around his throat, squeezing tightly until he was choking and clawing at the magic uselessly. Irsa's tiny chubby fist clenched tighter, and the tentacle reacted to the unconscious order, making the man's eyes roll back into his head.

"Irsa," her mother shouted weakly, dragging herself across the sand towards her daughter. Her trembling fingers, clutching Irsa's wrist, drawing the girl's attention away from the man. "Let him go," she gasped.

"He hurt you," Irsa whispered. Her chubby fist shuddered, refusing to release her hold on the man. "You're going to die, mama," her voice shook.

Hali nodded in agreement. "Yes. I am. But you have to let him go."

"Why?" The man had lost consciousness, but in her fury, Irsa's magic refused to let him go.

"Because this power is a gift." Hali coughed, blood seeping from her lips into the water around her face. "You can do great things with it."

"I don't care!" She shouted furiously. Why couldn't her mother see? Why couldn't she understand? Irsa needed to avenge her. She needed to make him pay for what he'd done!

"Death—" Hali coughed again, a soft wheeze leaving her as her lids seemed to grow heavier. Each breath became a struggle, as her mother fought to stay awake. "It will taint your power. After you kill someone with it, it'll never be the same. Don't let him ruin it. He's not worth it."

Irsa shook her head, her grip loosening as her mother peeled her fingers back one by one. "But Mama—"

"For me," Hali begged softly, clinging to her wrist. "Please, you must promise, for me?"

Irsa's whipped from side to side. She couldn't make that promise. Not now, maybe never.

"Promise me," her mother insisted.

The little girl's shoulders sagged, and she released the man. Her power dissipated into the water, allowing the unconscious man to sink down onto the sand. "Okay mama, I promise," she whispered brokenly.

Hali nodded, taking one last rattling breath before her fingers let go of Irsa's wrist and she too sank to the ocean floor. Irsa sank down into the sand beside her. She gripped her mother's pale hand between her own, sobbing.

The sea grew quiet around them. At some point, the man regained his senses and made off with his bounty, but Irsa didn't stop him this time. Instead, she cradled her mother's hand in her lap, sniffling for a long time. When at last she had cried herself out, she rose and mounted one of the seahorses. Irsa took one more look at her mother's lifeless form, then started the trek to the village.

An hour later brought her to the edge of Tjena, where Irsa grabbed the first royal soldier she saw and relayed all the events.

His brown eyes grow wide and nodded. "Don't you worry little miss, we will bring you mother home," he murmured soothingly, gesturing over her shoulder to a small group of soldiers. "Where do you live?"

Irsa somehow mumbled directions to her house and allowed him to lead her home. In the silence of an empty household—her father must have had a meeting—Irsa crawled into her bed and fell asleep.

Chapter Three

What felt like months later—but was merely a handful of days—Irsa and her father sat down for the third silent breakfast in a row. There came a knock at the door. When Calix didn't rise to answer it, Irsa grumbled. "I'll get it." She tossed a gauzy napkin over the clams on her plate and rose from the table.

Irsa opened the front door to reveal a be-speckled little mer about her age, with tangled muted blue hair and brown eyes. "Irsa of Tjena?" The girl asked, her tone sounding like she'd repeated the phrase over and over just to be sure she got it right.

"Yes, that's me," Irsa answered, her spine straightening. She eyed the slightly taller girl, wearily.

"I'm Janette," the girl announced, holding out a pale green hand. When Irsa just blinked at her in response, Janette frowned a little. Then she seemed to realize something and added, "I'm here under orders from the Council."

Irsa blinked a moment longer, processing what the girl had just said to her. "Oh—uh—would you like to come inside for some breakfast?"

"Yes. please." Janette chirped. She wasted no time swimming past Irsa into the house.

"This way," Irsa murmured, leading Janette back towards the dining room. Her father had already vacated his chair, leaving his half-empty plate behind. A sting like a jellyfish settled into Irsa's chest, but she ignored it. The pair of girls settled at the table and began to eat. Irsa waited with bated breath as Janette ate her way through an entire tray of fish egg and seaweed wraps.

"It is quite the thing, you know," Janette started, seeming to pick up from some train of thought she hadn't voiced.

"What is?" Irsa prompted.

Janette blinked at Irsa from behind her spectacles for a moment in confusion. It would seem Janette didn't realize Irsa didn't know what she was talking about. "Oh, the whole sea witch community is in a tizzy," she offered finally, licking a bit of crab custard from her thumb. When this didn't elicit the response she'd hoped for, Janette continued. "They're saying you are the strongest witch they've seen in nearly a century," she whispered conspiratorially.

Black eyes blinked at the other girl, shock registering on Irsa's young face. "I am?"

"You don't believe me?" Janette asked, affronted.

What was she supposed to say? She couldn't call Janette a liar, that would be rude. But she also didn't believe this nonsense about being the most powerful sea witch Alon had seen in nearly a century. Neither of her parents were very magical. Irsa's father had a little power of compulsion—enough to get him into trouble. And her mother—when she had been alive—had often struggled to heat a proper pot of tea. Less magic than a jellyfish, really. So how could she be so powerful? "No," she finally responded.

"No, she says," Janette muttered to herself, reaching for another wrap. How many had that been? Irsa had long ago lost count. "Well, it's the truth, it's why they sent me," she offered primly, sitting up straighter in her chair as if Irsa ought to be impressed by what an honor that was—Irsa wasn't.

"Right," Irsa mumbled, pushing her plate away from her.

"They're all fighting over you. Every witch from here to Malm wants you as their apprentice. I've even heard talk that some from the next kingdom over are vying for you," the girl continued with no prompting from Irsa. Janette stabbed the water in front of Irsa with the blunt knife in her hand. "Granted, King Hemnes would never let that happen. He'd be a fool to give up such talent to Vassviken. But you mark my words, you're quite something missy."

Irsa nodded disbelievingly, letting her companion chatter on and on about sea witch gossip. Janette threw around names of other witches, none of which Irsa recognized, but she continued to half-listen to the chatter. If nothing else, it was nice to have some company for the first time in days.

"DELIBERATIONS ARE DRAGGING ON, AND ON," Janette complained one afternoon a fortnight later as she ate her way through a plate of jellyfish sandwiches. "I hope to have an answer for you soon."

"It's all right, really," Irsa insisted. "I have other things to worry about right now."

And she did. While her future hung in the balance—with her grandmother long since dead—Irsa was left to plan her mother's funeral. She hardly saw her father except for the occasional "meetings" he'd mutter on his way out the door.

Irsa thanked Poseidon for Aislin, who helped her through every step of the process. At ten years old, she should not have been planning her mother's funeral, but she tried not to think of it.

"The whole village has turned up," Aislin whispered to Irsa, reaching over to take her hand as they floated on the edge of the deep dark valley where the merfolk of Alon buried their dead.

"They all loved her," Irsa murmured back, taking what comfort she could from Aislin's hand in hers as they lowered Hali's lifeless form down into the darkness.

Long after the ceremony, Irsa and Aislin floated there, hand in hand. "You'll see her again," Aislin promised. "She's too good to have only lived once. She'll be reincarnated." Her words were steady and sure.

Irsa sniffled, her free hand lifting to scrub at her face. "Poseidon willing," she whispered.

"No, Amphitrite willing," Aislin responded fiercely, giving her friend's hand another squeeze.

Silence settled between them, and Irsa felt herself holding her breath for fear she'd ruin the moment. "When do you leave?" She asked finally.

Aislin's brilliant green eyes turned towards her friend, and she smiled softly. "Two days. But I'm not going far. The seamstress they've apprenticed me to is just in the next village. I'll still see you plenty."

"Promise?"

"Swear," Aislin promised, her chubby hand squeezing Irsa's tightly again. "I won't leave you Irsa."

Irsa nodded. Her black eyes flicked back to the blackness of the crag before them. "Goodbye, mother," she whispered. Her pale fingers lifted to her lips, and she blew a kiss to the emptiness. Then she allowed Aislin to lead her to the only waiting carriage and home once more.

Chapter Four

It was another six months before Irsa heard any more of the Council's deliberations. She had wondered if perhaps they didn't want her after all when Janette appeared at her doorstep one afternoon. Janette looked more jittery than ever before and clutched desperately in her pale green fingers was a scroll.

"Would you like to come in for tea? Father isn't home, but I've made it up myself," Irsa offered politely to which the girl nodded eagerly. With a deep breath, Irsa floated back to let Janette enter the house.

They settled at the great coral table in the dining room with the tea things spread before them. Janette sipped from her teacup primly, the scroll floating in her lap. Irsa tried not to let the silence bother her, but she could feel the tension building. There was news. Janette had it and was being purposefully aloof.

After what felt like an hour of silence, Irsa'd had enough. "There is news," she said directly. It was not a question. She had waited long enough for this day. She wasn't about to wait a moment longer because Janette wanted to build the suspense.

"There is news," Janette confirmed, her hand falling to the scroll in her lap to clutch it once more.

"Well?" Irsa asked, irritation lacing her tone.

Janette bit her lower lip and then smiled brilliantly at her. "You've been assigned," she all but squealed causing Irsa to wince. Janette's green hand tightened further around the scroll. It crinkled in protest.

Irsa quirked one gray brow. Now nearly eleven, the little girl had seen enough of the world to not care one whit for such childish excitement. "Am I supposed to guess who my master will be, or are you prepared to tell me?"

This attitude did nothing to sober Janette, who was practically bobbing in her seat. Behind the thick spectacles, Janette's eyes shimmered in delight. "Oh, I suppose I could tell you," she muttered evasively. When Irsa cut her an impatient look, Janette giggled. Then she unfurled the scroll and held it out for Irsa to examine.

Irsa's black eyes trailed over the page, searching for the name of the witch who was to be her master. When she settled on it, her brows knitted. "Calypso?"

Janette gasped at her confusion. "You don't know who the Lady Calypso is?"

"No..." Irsa shifted awkwardly in her seat, as if she were being judged for her lack of knowledge.

"Really, child, do you know nothing?" Janette clicked her tongue disapprovingly as if Irsa were only a wee babe.

"My father never agreed with seeing sea witches for anything—I've never met one." Irsa's cheeks heated in shame. Already, she was grossly under prepared for the life ahead of her.

Another exaggerated gasp, Irsa wondered if Janette weren't better suited for acting than magic. "The Lady

Calypso is the highest-ranked sea witch in all of Alon! It's widely rumored that she is, in fact, the most powerful witch in the entire ocean!" Janette's excitement had quite gotten the better of her, and now she was muttering quickly. "King Hemnes himself has tried, on many occasions, to convince her to be the palace sea witch, but she refused. Young witches dream of being Calypso's apprentice."

Envy laced Janette's tone as she babbled on, and Irsa was almost positive that at one-point Janette had dreamed of being Calypso's apprentice. It would seem the girl hadn't made the cut. Irsa was a little guilty for that. She'd never even dreamed of being a witch, and it seemed that's all Janette had ever wanted. "Oh," Irsa muttered unenthusiastically.

"Oh? Oh!" Janette grumbled, rolling her eyes behind her spectacles. "Do you know what this means Irsa?"

"No," Irsa admitted softly.

"Calypso hasn't taken on an apprentice in nearly two hundred years! You should be ecstatic! This is the highest honor that can be paid to a young sea witch." Janette informed her. Perhaps hoping to stir some excitement in Irsa.

Irsa felt pressured to answer, but she didn't feel any such thing. It was hard to be excited about something that one did not wholly understand. "I suppose I am," she murmured.

Janette nodded finally and moved on with things. The conversation moved into more sea witch gossip that Irsa didn't understand nor care about. She didn't know any of those people, but she let Janette talk herself out as they enjoyed their tea.

Afterward, Irsa led Janette to the door. "Oh I almost forgot," Janette muttered, opening the scroll once more. "Sign it." She pointed to the line at the bottom of the parchment and holding out a tiny squid that looked absolutely terrified.

Irsa took the squid in her hand so she could scribble her name on the line. A gasp left her when the ink glowed a violent shade of red, and something in her stomach twisted in an unfamiliar dread. "What was that?"

Janette shrugged. "Magically binding, and all that. It's a requirement. Here are your instructions." She held out another scroll and then turned to leave. "Good luck, Irsa. I know that it says you don't have to be there for a month but... I wouldn't keep Lady Calypso waiting. She can get terribly testy."

Then Janette left, swimming down the street back towards wherever she came from. Irsa wasn't sure what witch Janette was apprenticed under, but she assumed she'd find out, eventually. She ducked her head to eye the instructions and gulped. A month. She had a month to pack up her life and move to the next village over to meet her mistress.

The only bright spot was that the village they assigned her to; the same one where Aislin had moved.

"I won't be alone," she whispered, turning back into the house and shutting the door.

Chapter Five

A month later found Irsa happily settled in Calypso's manor on the outskirts of a village much too small to be the address of a sea witch as prolific as Calypso.

"This place is so big," Aislin gasped in surprise as Irsa led her back to the small table in the kitchen that Calypso had told her she could use for their afternoon tea. "And it's just you two living here?" She asked.

Irsa shrugged a little. "And some servants," she added.

"Wow," Aislin muttered to herself.

Silence reigned as a maid poured each of the young mergirls tea. They sipped quietly; the maid weighing the small table down with all manner of treats. "Will there be anything else, Miss Irsa?" The girl—not much older than Irsa and Aislin herself—asked.

"No, thank you, Bronte. That will be all right." Irsa murmured kindly.

The girl bobbed a gentle curtsy, spun in a flurry of bubbles, and disappeared into another part of the house. Aislin, thank Poseidon, waited till that moment to giggle obnoxiously. "Goodness, Irsa, you're like a princess," she gushed.

Her friend snorted, rolling black eyes in exasperation. "I am nothing of the kind Aislin. I'll leave that to you." She teased softly, which drew another soft giggle from Aislin. "So," Irsa said, lifting a tiny sea cucumber sandwich to her lips. "What do I owe this pleasure?"

Aislin shifted uncomfortably in her seat for a moment before releasing a soft sigh. "You will not like this," she whispered.

Black eyes narrowed as Irsa watched her friend more closely. "Out with it," she demanded.

Aislin's bright green eyes fell to the table before them, struggling with the words she knew Irsa needed to hear. "I heard some gossip from Tjena," she hedged softly. Irsa quirked one gray brow to prompt her onward. Inhaling deeply, Aislin continued, "Lansa has moved in with your father."

Pain shot through Irsa's chest, her breath coming up short suddenly. "Mother hasn't even been dead a year," she whispered.

"That's not all." Aislin's voice was soft and soothing. "There is talk that perhaps she's expecting."

Irsa lifted her hand to clutch at the lacy tunic over her heart. It hurt, why did it hurt so much? She supposed she was hurting on behalf of her mother. If Hali were alive, this news would kill her. Or perhaps it was that her father had found himself a replacement family so quickly. "How long?" Irsa choked.

Wide green eyes blinked at Irsa for a moment. Then Aislin answered in a soft, pained tone, "the gossip is that this was going on before we lost Hali."

"Meetings," Irsa muttered with a scoff before falling quiet.

Aislin allowed Irsa time to process, focusing her attention entirely on a kelp sandwich between her fingers. Irsa loved her dear friend for that; Aislin always knew when to be quiet. Nothing more needed saying, they both knew that.

After several minutes, Irsa regained control of her racing mind and muttered almost embarrassedly—wanting nothing more than to change the subject. "It would seem I will soon be in the market for a ball gown."

A gasp fell from Aislin's lips. "And you'll want me to make it, I'll make you the most beautiful ball gown in all of Alon," she whispered desperately, reaching forward to take her friend's hand in a grasp so tight it may have crushed bone.

Irsa didn't mind. "Nothing too extravagant, it's just for Council meetings," she chided gently, her black eyes flicking over Aislin's face as the redhead nodded too quickly.

"Of course, of course," Aislin agreed. "It will be quite understated." Her head bobbed in another quick nod.

Irsa bit her lip to keep from laughing, and the conversation fell into talks of fine jellyfish silks, and flounder taffetas and many fripperies Irsa did not care for nor understand. That was Aislin's world, and she would be happy to let her friend dress her.

That evening, as Irsa lay in the center of the soft bed Calypso had given her, her dark eyes stared up at the gauzy canopy hiding the ceiling from view. Irsa's mind went to her mother and the earnest look in her eyes when Hali had made her promise to use her magic for good.

She needed to make something of herself. She needed to

be the best sea witch Alon had ever seen. She needed to make her mother proud. There seemed to be no choice. Either Irsa made her mother proud, or Hali died in vain.

THE NEXT TWO years of Irsa's life brought endless events and lessons. Calypso showered her in beautiful gowns and fancy food and showed her off like a prized seahorse at every available opportunity.

It was at one such party that Irsa began to see Calypso for what she really was. The now thirteen-year-old sea witch had spent her week studying hard for an upcoming test with the Council, and then Calypso insisted they had to go out to some such party. The lord who was hosting it didn't seem at all interested in what Irsa could do, his only interest lay in having the powerful young witch at his party.

"Show them your light," Calypso instructed gently, her wide smile showing off a row of shark-like teeth.

Irsa blinked up at her mistress, dark eyes rimmed in bruises of tiredness from having studied the entire night before. "Mistress, perhaps another time," she whispered roughly, then yawned into the back of her hand.

Until then, Calypso had been distant but kind to Irsa. "Child, show them your light," she instructed again, but this time the gentleness edged in anger. Just out of the corner of Irsa's eyes, she could see Calypso's crimson magic beginning to glow around her.

Irsa nodded, letting her light flow from her in brilliant purple tentacles much to the delight of the small crowd they had drawn. Only she and Calypso knew that they were perhaps not as bright, nor as alive as they ought to have been, but in her exhaustion, Irsa decided they would have to be good enough.

That evening as they headed home, Irsa pressed her face to the cold glass of the carriage window. She closed her eyes, allowing herself rest for the first time in over a week.

"Useless girl," Calypso growled from the seat beside her.

Irsa lifted her head to look at her mistress blearily. "What?" She asked, confused.

"I said, you pitiful, foolish, useless girl," Calypso hissed. "Do you know what a fool you made me look? And in front of the Lord Eryx's guests no less!"

"But Mistress, I was just tired from—" Her explanation cut off by a hard slap to Irsa's pale cheek. A sob left her throat, her hand flying up to hold her stinging face. "I'm sorry, Mistress," she whispered brokenly.

The raven-haired witch nodded, and they spent the rest of the ride in silence.

It had been an anomaly, Irsa convinced herself. The bruise on her cheek was the product of a bad night. Calypso had been under a lot of stress and had snapped.

"Your tea, mistress," Irsa whispered, setting the tray carefully onto Calypso's driftwood desk. She poured her Mistress a cup and set it beside the papers on the desk.

"Thank you, Irsa," Calypso muttered distractedly. Her bright blue eyes didn't even bother to leave the papers for a long moment until she noticed that the girl hadn't left her office yet. "What is it Irsa," she asked.

Irsa floated in front of her Mistress's desk, her pale hands twisting behind her back. She wore on her lower lip and took a breath. "I was just wondering what you'd like me to work on this evening, Mistress?"

Calypso's glowing blue eyes finally lifted from the papers and softened at the sight of the little girl. "Come here, child," she cooed, extending her hand to Irsa. Irsa nodded quickly and swam over to her Mistress. She took the offered hand in her own and let Calypso give her a soft squeeze.

"Yes, Mistress?" She asked softly.

Calypso lifted her free hand to brush over Irsa's still bruised cheek. "You know I'm sorry that I hurt you, don't you Irsa?"

Irsa blinked at her Mistress for a moment, unsure what she was to do with the soft words. A piece of her wanted to yell at Calypso and tell her that sorry wouldn't cut it. While another part—arguably the part that missed her mother still—wanted to lean into that soft touch and accept what Calypso was giving her. It was the lonely part that won out. "Yes, Mistress," Irsa whispered with a nod. Calypso watched her expectantly for a moment before Irsa admitted softly, "I am sorry, as well, Mistress. I should have done better."

Calypso nodded, satisfied with the apology. "It's all right, my dear, you are still growing as a young witch. And I have been working you particularly hard as of late, haven't I?"

Irsa squeezed Calypso's hand. "No, Mistress, I can handle all of it. I promise I'll do better in the future," she swore softly. She needed nothing more in that moment than to please Calypso. To convince her Irsa could and would do anything to be the very best apprentice there was.

Calypso clucked her tongue gently, shaking her head.

"None of that, my dear. I'll hear no such protests." She murmured, taking Irsa's chin in her hand to turn her face so she could get a better look at the bruise. "I'll give you a spell to heal it more quickly. I want you to practice that until it's gone, yes?"

"Yes, Mistress," Irsa agreed softly.

Calypso smiled gently at her, leaning in to press a kiss to the little girl's forehead. "Good. Now, I think in the meantime, you ought to have a little fun. Shouldn't you?"

"If it won't take too much from my studies, ma'am," she whispered.

The raven-haired witch clucked her tongue softly. "Nonsense, my dear, all work and no play makes Irsa a dull girl. Besides, you're still a child. You deserve some fun. Why not have your little friend over for tea?"

At the mention of Aislin, Irsa perked right up, seeing her dear friend was the closest she got to home, and she'd do anything to have more of it. "Really, Miss?"

"Yes, just stay in the kitchen. You won't be in the way there. I won't have my household disrupted by your social life. Do you understand, child?" She quirked a black brow over her glowing blue eyes in question but seemed dissatisfied when the little girl nodded quickly. "I need to hear you say the words, Irsa." Calypso's tone held a note of warning now.

"Yes, Mistress. Aislin and I won't be any trouble to the staff. We will not cause a disruption," Irsa muttered.

With a curt nod, the sea witch jerked her hand from the little girl's face and returned to the papers on her desk. "You are dismissed, child."

"Yes, Mistress," Irsa repeated automatically. Then she spun in the water and left with a flurry of bubbles in her wake.

Tales of a Sea Witch

IRSA PUT all of her focus into the healing magic her Mistress had taught her. She wanted to prove this hadn't been a mistake. She also didn't particularly want Aislin seeing the bruise and misinterpreting it. That would not do.

When the day finally came for tea, Irsa had wished away the bruise until it was nothing more than a shadow on her cheek. So light, in fact, that she was sure not even her nearest and dearest Aislin would see it. Or at least she hoped not.

The soft chime of the magical bell at the door alerted Irsa to Aislin's arrival just as she finished laying out the tea things. "Oh, she's early," Irsa muttered to herself. "Why must she always be early?

Still, she went to open the door and was happy when Aislin flung herself at the gray-haired mergirl. They squeezed each other tightly. Irsa absorbed every ounce of comfort that her friend could provide and hoped to return it in full if not double.

"I'm sorry I'm so early," Aislin murmured when she pulled back, her green eyes alight with excitement. "I was so excited to see you."

She lifted one tanned hand to smooth over her friend's cheek, brushing the mostly healed bruise. Pain laced through Irsa's face, and she winced. "Careful," she whispered.

Aislin's eyes widened in panic as she searched her friend's face and found the bruise. "Irsa, you're hurt! What happened?" She held the cheek more tenderly.

"It's all right, it's already almost healed." Irsa did her best to push it aside, smiling softly at her friend. "Trust me, I'm fine."

"You didn't answer my question," Aislin insisted, her

intense green eyes pinning her friend to the spot. "Who did this to you?"

Irsa bit the tip of her tongue, she hated to lie to her friend, but she knew she had to. Aislin wouldn't understand what had happened. She would assume the worst. "It was an accident; I swam into something—" The excuse sounded weak even to her ears. "A door," she finished lamely. "Not something to worry yourself over." She pulled back from Aislin's gentle touch and insistent probing. "Now come on, tea's getting cold." Spinning in the water, she swam back through the house to the kitchen without another word.

Chapter Six

That was not the last beating Calypso would give her young apprentice. The cycle that began that day continued for five years. Irsa upset her Mistress; Calypso lashed out, then the witch would apologize and make it up to her. Irsa hid it as best she could from her friend, but Aislin always seemed to know. But overall, life went on.

The young sea witch's sixteenth birthday arrived with little fuss, but Aislin insisted on a shopping trip, which is what found Irsa floating in front of the seamstress shop, peering in the window. She waved at Aislin, who waved back, a bright smile lighting her freckled face. Over the years Aislin had grown ever more beautiful, and every time she smiled, Irsa's heart did a strange somersault.

"You weren't waiting long, were you?" Aislin asked breathlessly. She slung a sharkskin satchel over her shoulder, examining her reflection in the glass for a moment as she fidgeted with her hair till it was just so.

"No, not long," Irsa murmured. Her eyes fixed on Aislin, entranced by the shimmering red locks. Irsa shook herself, then scowled at her friend in the glass. "Are you going to float there and fiddle with your hair all day, or are we going shopping?"

Bright green eyes flicked to Irsa in the reflection before Aislin giggled softly. "We're going shopping. Come along!" She took Irsa's smaller hand in hers, and they were off.

The two girls went from shop to shop, browsing, and trying on, and giggling for hours. Irsa's belly hurt from laughing, but she didn't let it stop her. It was nice to be with Aislin. To be how things once were when they were children. Yet, it wasn't the same. No, every brush of Aislin's hand, every smile on her lips, made Irsa's heart flip-flop. She couldn't explain the feeling, nor did she try to. It didn't matter, not so long as they were both happy, together, and having fun.

"Race you to the bookshop," Aislin called over her shoulder, already swimming at break-neck speed down the street in a flurry of bubbles.

"No fair! You got a head start!" Irsa shouted after her, laughing. Then she too took off, using her magic to push herself harder, faster. Soon she was neck and neck with Aislin. She grabbed the red-haired mer by the waist and pulled her in close. They spun in the water, bubbles swirling around them. Their laughter mingled until their spinning stopped, and the two mergirls floated in the middle of the street, breathlessly staring into each other's flushed faces. Irsa's her heart skittered along in her chest, her fingers seeming to burn where they gripped Aislin's narrow waist. "Caught you," she whispered.

"Yeah, you did," Aislin whispered back. Then she leaned in closer—her eyes squeezed shut—and pressed a chaste kiss to Irsa's lips. It was all at once awkward and sweet, leaving Irsa's head spinning and heart thumping. She hardly had time to respond before Aislin pulled her lips away, her red lashes fluttering open, and a deep red flush settling into her freckled cheeks. "Happy Birthday Irsa."

"Happy Birthday Aislin," Irsa responded. "I mean, I don't mean Happy Birthday. It's not your birthday for another two weeks! Oh, that was stupid," Irsa stammered, her cheeks heating brightly.

Aislin laughed happily, pressed a kiss to her friend's nose, and pulled back entirely. "Come on; I want to buy you something extra special from the bookstore!"

Irsa nodded dumbly. She let Aislin take her hand and lead her into the store. "Just no princess stories," she muttered.

"No, no princess stories," Aislin agreed with a giggle.

Instead, Aislin dragged her to the magic section. Irsa blinked, looking up the shelves in confusion. "What do I need with this? Calypso has a whole library of all the magic books I'd ever need." She plucked one up, flipping it open to eye the spells dubiously.

"Just in case," Aislin shrugged evasively. "I thought maybe you'd like something for yourself, that wasn't Calypso's. You know, start building your own library for when you've finished your apprenticeship." She plucked a tome from the shelf, reading over the title on the spine.

"These are expensive, Aislin. I can wait to start my library," Irsa protested weakly. Still, her hands itched for all the books before her—to hoard them away like a crab does dead things.

"Nonsense, it's your birthday. What about this one?" She asked, holding out a book of poisons and healing potions. "You can always use some extra healing magic with how clumsy you are," Aislin added, helpfully. Aislin had accepted the lies about Irsa's clumsiness, but Irsa knew that she didn't quite believe them. Still, they didn't talk about it. Things were simpler that way.

"I don't need a book of poisons, though. Don't they have one with just healing magic?"

Aislin shrugged. "You might need the poisons; you don't know."

Irsa quirked one gray brow at her friend. Her lips twitch downward suspiciously. "What would I need with them?"

"I don't know, just in case, I guess. You never know Irsa. Besides, look, the cover is pretty! It's red!" She gestured wildly to the embossed red cover. Irsa had to admit; it was beautiful. "Come on, just let me buy it for you."

"All right," Irsa rolled her eyes. She followed Aislin to the front. There, her friend paid for the book and stuffed it into her bag without another word about it. They headed into the street, hand in hand.

"Ooh. You know what you need," Aislin whispered, a little smile tugging at her lips.

Irsa looked at her suspiciously—only half wanting to know what Aislin was on about now—but she asked, anyway. "What?"

"A haircut!" Aislin's voice was loud with excitement. Irsa decided not to fight it. She let the other girl drag her off to a tiny salon.

An hour later found Irsa staring at a very changed reflection of herself. The little girl with long gray hair had been replaced with a young merwoman. Her hair was short, cut to about an inch from her scalp, making the lines of her face look sharper. "You look amazing," Aislin squealed loudly, kissing her cheek.

Irsa wrinkled her nose, leaning close to the mirror to get a better look. "Really?"

"Definitely," Aislin nodded firmly.

Irsa nodded, her lips twitching into a little smile. Her

black eyes flicked to the window to see the water beyond growing darker. "Aislin, it's getting late," she whispered. "Calypso will wonder where I am. I wasn't supposed to be gone more than a few hours."

"Oh, all right," Aislin whispered, her shoulders sagging. "Can I swim you home?"

Irsa shook her head. "No, that's a good idea. I'll see you next week for tea?" She rose from the chair, swimming over it to hug her friend tightly. "Thank you for today. It was the best birthday ever."

"Yes, I'll see you for tea. Have a safe swim home." Aislin kissed her cheek. "I'll pay for your hair, go on, I don't want Calypso mad at you."

Irsa nodded and spun in the water. She swam from the salon, and down the street as fast as she could, her chest heaving. It took her an hour and a half to reach Calypso's manor on the outskirts of town. The water had grown almost inky black in that time. "Poseidon please, let her be asleep," Irsa whispered a prayer to the god of the sea before going into the house.

All seemed quiet and dark within the manor of Lady Calypso. Her young apprentice made her way silently through the halls, praying to Poseidon that everyone was asleep. If she were lucky Calypso would already be in bed, and Irsa would escape the thrashing her Mistress thought she deserved.

The door to Calypso's study sat before a broad slope leading up to the bedrooms. Irsa could see no light shining through the crack and breathed a little easier.

Past the door, and almost to the steps, Irsa's heart settled in her chest. Calypso was asleep she was—

"Irsa," Calypso's voice was sharp.

"Yes, Mistress?" Irsa asked, her heart hammering in her chest.

"Get in here, now," her Mistress growled, and Irsa's heart stopped altogether.

"Yes, Mistress," she whispered, ducking her head low. Swimming into the office, the young sea-witch tried to make herself as small as possible. Irsa had learned long ago that if she made herself small enough, Calypso had a hard time hitting anything vital. Inside, the office was lit only by a single jellyfish lamp casting Calypso's features in a sharper light. "I'm sorry I'm late Mistress," Irsa whispered. "I'll make it up to you. I'll clean the library and make sure the books are in order twice this month. I'll work up all the stupid love charms. I'll—"

"You'll sit down," Calypso commanded, using compulsion to force Irsa into one of the seats before her desk. Then the sea witch rose from her chair, long ruby-red tail, and gauzy dorsal fins fluttering around her dangerously. "This day marks the end of your acquaintance with that... girl," Calypso's sharp teeth gnashed, daring Irsa to go against her.

Black eyes went wide. Irsa's face paled, pain settling into her chest. The end? "I'm sorry, Mistress, I don't think I understand you. What, girl?" Irsa asked, hoping she had misheard. Maybe there had just been a misunderstanding.

The jellyfish lamp burned brighter, Calypso's electric blue eyes sizzling with it in a warning. "You were seen today," she hissed.

"S-s-seen?" Irsa asked, her mind flashing to the kiss she'd shared with Aislin. It had been in plain view in the middle of the street, but it had been so quick she didn't think anyone would have noticed. Her heart hammered in her chest.

"Yes, seen," Calypso repeated. "Half the town is already talking about the filthy kiss you shared in the middle of the street today. By morning, the other half will know. I can't have my apprentice be taking part in such disgusting behavior." Her words dripped with revulsion. "Not only is it repugnant—it is illegal by Alon law to have such relations."

"We're just friends," Irsa argued weakly. "Aislin is my friend, not anything else. We weren't doing anything illegal! We're friends!" Her words became more vehement the longer she spoke, but even to herself, she heard the lie. Aislin hadn't been just Irsa's friend for quite some time.

"Now that friendship is over," Calypso ordered. Magic sizzled in the surrounding water, threatening to boil them both alive.

"No, it's not." Irsa rose from the chair, fury heating her cheeks. She had never—not once—raised her voice to Calypso. Every beating she had taken with her head bowed in submission. Every telling-off she'd accepted. But this, this was too much. Irsa loved Aislin, had loved her for her entire life, and a life without her friend would be barren. Devoid of meaning. She would have nothing left. She couldn't and wouldn't sever her tie to Aislin. "I will not stop being friends with her just because of gossip. And that's all this is, gossip!"

The sting of the witch's magic came suddenly and sharply. Calypso wielded her power like a whip, lashing first Irsa's tail, then her face. "You forget, child, you belong to me. We have a contract." Her voice was low and threatening. "You are mine until you complete your training. Until then, your will belongs to me, and you will do as I bid you."

Another lash across Irsa's cheek left it open and bleeding. The young girl winced, squeezing her eyes shut. "You can't force me to stop being friends with someone."

A slow smirk split Calypso's lips, showing two rows of

dangerously pointed shark-like teeth. "No, I can't force you to end your friendship. But I can end it for you."

Black eyes widened, Irsa wasn't sure what Calypso meant by that, but she was sure she would not like it. "H-h-how?"

A mean glint had settled into those eerily cruel eyes. Irsa's Mistress would enjoy watching her squirm. "Tonight, you will stay in this room—to think about what you've done."

"You can't—"

"Ah, ah, ah," Calypso chided. Her mouth twisting into a cruel smile. "I think you'll find I can do many a thing. You signed that contract, little fish, your body—at least—is bound to me." Irsa's heart hammered in her chest again, the water around her turning icy cold as Calypso's magic turned frigid. "When I say stay put, you will."

Shimmering letters snaked through the water towards Irsa, whispering, *'Stay put. Stay put. Stay put.'* over and over. They lassoed around her middle—tightening enough to push the water from her lungs—and forced her down into the chair again. Once there, they tied her to it, and as much as Irsa struggled, she could not move.

"Goodnight, little guppy," Calypso cooed in an icy tone. She pressed a lingering kiss to Irsa's forehead before disappearing through the door.

Irsa struggled against the bindings for what seemed like hours. Her amethyst magic writhed around her to break their hold. When that failed, she reached for a pair of sheers on the desk and tried to cut her way out. Nothing. There was no escape. She had exhausted herself and every plan of escape she had, so she let her head hang forward and drifted into a restless sleep.

Chapter Seven

*M*orning light filtered harsh and bright through the sea urchin silk curtains of Calypso's office. Irsa blinked awake slowly, her head thick and groggy from a night of little sleep. There, sitting at the desk, was Calypso, looking for all the sea like she had slept like a newborn mer. Irsa was so tired; she couldn't find it within herself to be annoyed at the cheerful face staring back at her.

"I have had your new room made up," Calypso announced sipping from the mug in between her fingers.

Irsa blinked at her blankly, the words registering slowly. "Wh-what?" She asked when confusion replaced exhaustion.

"Come," the single word snaked through the water, its power tugging Irsa from the chair to follow Calypso. They swam through the foyer and bustling kitchen to a little door just beyond. There was a tiny room just barely large enough for the cot of driftwood and seaweed inside. Beside the makeshift bed rested a battered crate turned on its lid. Otherwise, the room was barren. "Welcome home,"

Calypso murmured, then shoved Irsa into the tiny room. "Make yourself comfortable, little guppy, you won't be leaving for some time."

Irsa spun just in time for the door slam shut. In the place of a knob burned a glowing red handprint. She was trapped, for the time being. With a deep exhale, Irsa settled onto the hard cot, burying her face in her hands.

"It can't be for much longer," she whispered thoughtfully. "Surely, I don't have much longer in my apprenticeship." Or at least, she hoped that was the case. Long fingers fell to brush over the satchel beside her on the bed. Calypso hadn't bothered with it, thankfully. She pulled the book from it, to run her fingers over the gold-embossed cover. Despite how it had ended, that had been the best birthday she'd ever had.

Flipping through the pages, she found a healing spell for her still oozing cheek. Irsa closed her eyes and reached for her magic. She struggled to call upon it in her sleep-deprived and weakened state. The soft glowing light felt so very far away, but she could draw enough power from it to at least stop the bleeding. When she had exhausted that effort, she leaned back on the cot and began to read.

Irsa sat in that tiny room for a very long time—the only sign of time passing was her growling belly, and how many pages she read in the book Aislin had bought her. Heat, that was her only warning that Calypso would join her. The room became hot right before the door flung open with a flurry of angry bubbles and red magic. She had enough time to tuck the book away before the bubbles cleared.

"How do you like your new room?" Calypso asked. That nasty gleam was still in her bright blue eyes. She was enjoying this far too much, and Irsa would not give her the satisfaction.

"It's fine, Mistress. I think I'll be comfortable here," Irsa responded, a cheeky grin tugging at her lips. It would only make things worse for her, she knew that, but she couldn't seem to stop herself.

The witch quirked one black brow, irritation making the muscle below her eye twitch. "No complaints?"

"None," Irsa replied. "Is it time for lessons?"

"Yes. Come along." Calypso spun and swam away, expecting Irsa to follow. They swam in silence to the large, open training room where all of Irsa's lessons had taken place. Glimmering red magic slammed the door behind Irsa, the sound rippling off the walls.

Irsa swallowed nervously but kept her chin held high. She would not show fear. "Where would you like me to start, Mistress?"

"Call upon your light," Calypso replied. She swam to flop down into a chair along the wall, watching with interest.

Irsa closed her black eyes and reached for the living thing within her that Calypso referred to as her light. That writhing, living thing inside of her was not always easy to call forth, for it was an animal of sorts. If not coaxed just right, it turned its back on Irsa and refused to come out. She knew that one day she and her magic would be as one. They would want the same things. That would come in time, Calypso had assured her.

"What's taking so long?" Calypso asked, obnoxiously, breaking Irsa's concentration and causing the glittering magic to retreat further.

"What?" Irsa asked in confusion. When she'd trained with Calypso before, she'd told Irsa that the first time she reached for the light in the day would be the hardest. It had gotten better, in time. Slowly, Irsa felt her magic bending to her will.

"We have been at this for years Irsa," Calypso growled.

"You should be able to do this in your sleep! What kind of useless witch can't even call upon her magic?"

Swallowing roughly, Irsa forced her voice to remain even. "You said it would take time and training. That's why I'm here—training."

"And you've had your training, where are the results?"

"Maybe if you hadn't been using my magic as a parlor trick to impress your friends for the last decade," Irsa snapped back at her. Anger heating her belly and the power within her growling to life.

Calypso's only reply was the lash of a glowing red whip, reopening the wound Irsa had just healed on her cheek. "Don't sass me, child! Again!" She shouted, one dark brow raising as if daring Irsa to contradict her again.

Irsa bit her tongue, ducked her head, and tried again. When she reached for that creature this time, she found a barrier between herself and her power. A thin sheet of something blocking her from tapping into it as she always had. She struggled against it, pushing until the barrier gave, and she could bring forth the tentacles of amethyst light. Calm and rightness washed over her as she bathed in that power.

"Now let it go, and begin again," Calypso ordered.

"Wh-what?" Irsa looked at her Mistress, her eyes watering from the brightness of the surrounding magic.

"Do as I say!" The witch's voice rippled, a warning on the tide.

Irsa nodded quickly, releasing the magic. It dissipated into the water, floating away on the current into nothingness. Then she began again. She lost track of time as her Mistress made her repeat the process over and over again. Each time her exhaustion and hunger made the barrier separating her from her power that much thicker.

They did not stop until a servant came to call them for

supper. Of which Irsa was served little more than a crust of stale sea urchin bread, and some jellyfish jam. Then Calypso ordered her to bed, and that was the end.

EVERY MORNING — FOR so many that Irsa lost count — Calypso would retrieve her from her small room before breakfast and keep her in the training room until well after supper. Every day, Irsa's magic slipped further and further away from her. That barrier between herself and it grew thicker, and she grew weaker. It wasn't just the lack of proper food or sleep; there was something else. Irsa could feel something else happening.

Relief came some months later when Calypso announced that she would go into the city for business.

"I'll be gone for a fortnight." Calypso's voice was soft. Her long, red-tinged hand lifted to brush one gleaming red fingernail down Irsa's cheek. "Behave yourself in my absence, little guppy."

"Yes, Mistress," Irsa whispered, her head bowed in submission.

The witch nodded, pulling her hand away from her apprentice. "You are not to leave the manor until I get back," she ordered, but there was no hint of the compulsion magic she had used recently. "Do you understand?"

"Yes, Mistress." Irsa nodded.

Without another word, Calypso swam into the carriage, and she was off. Behind her was a trail of bubbles and swirling sand. As the distance between herself and her mistress grew, a weight lifted from her slowly. A lightness settled into her chest that hadn't been there in some months, and the young apprentice breathed a sigh of relief.

Then she spun in the water to head back inside.

Moments later she snuck from the manor, a flowing black cloak shrouding her from head to fin. It was a risk, but Irsa didn't think twice about taking it.

With her weariness, the swim into town took Irsa longer than she would have liked. Still, she floated in front of the seamstress shop soon enough. The bell over the door chimed, followed by a voice from the back room calling, "We'll be with you in a moment."

Irsa's lips twitched into a soft smile at the sound of Aislin's voice. "No problem," she called back.

"Irsa?" Aislin asked, peaking around the corner. Her freckled face lit up with a bright smile at the sight of her friend. "Irsa," she exclaimed, swimming to her, and wrapping her in a bone-crushing hug.

Irsa could hardly be bothered that it cut off the water to her lungs. She focused on the warmth of her friend holding her close, warmth spread through her, and she sighed. She hadn't known just how cold she was until that moment. "Great Poseidon, that's wonderful," she whispered.

Aislin held her for perhaps a moment longer than others would deem appropriate before pulling back to beam at her friend. Bright green eyes flicked over Irsa's face, and then the smile fell. "What happened to you?" She whispered.

"What do you mean?" Irsa lifted her hands to press to her face. She had healed the lashes on her cheeks; surely, there could be no sign of Calypso's abuse. "I'm fine," she insisted.

Aislin's frown deepened, her eyes growing worried. "Irsa, you are not fine," she near choked, looking as if she were on the verge of tears. She took Irsa's hands in hers and tugged her gently into one of the dressing rooms along the far wall. There, she forced Irsa in front of a mirror, bringing the hood away from her face.

Black eyes fell upon the mer in the mirror, drawing a

gasp from Irsa. That person looking back at her looked wholly unlike herself. The girl in the mirror was a pitiful, drawn excuse for a mer. Grey-brown cheek had been hallowed out—as if with a clam scooper—from starvation. Darkness ringed her eyes from lack of sleep. "That's not me," the girl in the mirror whispered in disbelief. The cloak rippled around her in the water to reveal that even Irsa's glimmering amethyst tail was a shadow of what it once was —now, a dull purple color, and much thinner.

"What has she done to you," Aislin demanded. Her hands gripped Irsa by the shoulders and forced her friend down onto a stool. "On your birthday you looked so happy and healthy." Red brows creased, her green eyes searching Irsa's face.

"How long has it been?" Irsa found her voice shaking. She wrapped her arms around her middle self-consciously, wanting to be as small as possible so that Aislin couldn't see her. Not out of fear, but shame. How had she allowed this to happen?

"Six months," Aislin answered, not bothering to ask why Irsa didn't know. She moved onto bent tail in the sand before her friend. Irsa let Aislin take her hands, forcing her to relinquish her hold of her middle. The softness of Aislin's hands, combined with the gentle squeeze, slowed Irsa's racing heart. "I'm going to go make you some tea. Don't move."

"Where are you going?" Irsa hated the way her voice broke.

"Just back into the break room, I won't be far," her friend assured her.

"C-c-can I come with you?" Irsa whispered. Black eyes watched as her fingers fiddled nervously atop her bent fin. Weak—that's what she was. She was weak.

Aislin let out a soft breath. She reached for those

wringing hands, giving them another firm squeeze. "Sure. Come on."

Irsa smiled weakly, letting Aislin tug her from the stool and back to the back room. Once there, Aislin pushed her down into a chair, and not long after placed a boiling cup of tea between her hands. "Thank you," Irsa murmured, her fingers wrapping around it to warm them.

"Drink," Aislin instructed. She sat across from her at the small table, a mug in her own hands. "It'll help you relax."

Aislin waited until Irsa had taken a few fortifying sips. Irsa's tired eyes closed, the warmth from the tea seeping down into her bones. It felt so good. She took another sip, letting her shoulders relax for perhaps the first time in six months.

Once Aislin seemed assured her friend was feeling a little better, she asked, "What happened?"

Black eyes opened to peer at Aislin, and Irsa sighed. "It's hard to explain."

"Try," her friend insisted.

With a rough swallow, Irsa did her best to explain. "My magic is so far away. There's something between us, or it's vanishing, and soon I'll have nothing left. And then—" A sob choked off the rest of her words.

"And then you'll die," Aislin whispered, finishing the thought for her. She was quiet for a long time; then she narrowed her green eyes, her full lips pressing into a narrow line. "She's done something to you."

Irsa frowned in confusion. "What?"

"She's put a spell on you of some kind, to separate you from your power. I wouldn't be surprised if she's draining you like a leech!" Aislin's hands balled into fists on the table as anger filled her.

"Aislin, I don't thin—"

Irsa tried to reason with her, but Aislin cut her off. "No. Irsa, you've been with her for six years now. You should be stronger, not weaker! You need to leave her."

"I can't," Irsa breathed out the words. "I signed a contract. She owns me until my apprenticeship has finished. At least two more years."

Red brows furrowed in thought, and Aislin chewed on her lower lip. "Then—" her voice lowered to a whisper. "We have to kill her."

"What," Irsa squawked. "We can't—" She too lowered her voice. "We can't kill Calypso."

Aislin took Irsa's hands, meeting her eyes firmly. "Irsa, we have to. If we don't get you out of that contract, you'll be dead before you finish your apprenticeship. I can't lose you."

"Maybe there is another way. A loophole," Irsa argued hopefully. "There has to be something."

Aislin inhaled deeply and nodded. "Then we'll look at the contract and see. Do you think you can find it?"

"Yes. Calypso is gone for a while—I have time to search."

"Try to find it before the end of the week," Aislin insisted.

Irsa's stomach twisted, but she agreed. It wouldn't be an easy task, but it needed to be done. Aislin was right; she didn't know how much longer she'd last with how things were.

***

WITH CALYPSO GONE, the staff had taken some much-needed time off. That meant when Irsa returned to the manor that evening, all was still and quiet. She could slip through the halls unbothered, and into Calypso's study unmolested. Once there, she lit the witch light and set to work.

Aislin had said to find the contract before the week was out, but Irsa didn't want to chance Calypso coming back before she had. She dove in headfirst. She searched for hours, digging through the clam-shell file cabinet against the wall.

After hours of searching, Irsa sat in the middle of the floor—her tail bent behind her—files laid out around her. The first signs of morning light filtered in through the windows, and she stilled in her fumbling to listen to the sounds of the house. Her breath caught in her throat, her heart all but stopping, ears straining for any sound of life. Amphitrite was on her side this day, the manor remained still as the grave.

She turned back to the files, each marked with a name. What she found inside them made Irsa's blood run cold. "I've got to show Aislin," she whispered. Scooping up the papers, Irsa made a mad dash for the door.

Irsa did not stop swimming until she reached the seamstress. It wasn't open yet. She banged on the door, her breath coming in ragged pants.

Aislin peaked out from the back room, her green eyes wide. When she saw who it was, she swam quickly to the door and let in her friend. "Irsa? What is it? Do you know what time it is? We aren't even open—"

Irsa pushed past her, cutting Aislin off mid-rant. "Look at this." She laid each file out on the table, running a hand through her short mussed gray hair.

Aislin blinked down at the files, not understanding the connection. "Those are Calypso's files on all of her apprentices," she intoned.

"No, not that—this," Irsa grumbled. She flipped each open to the very last page.

"Death certificates?" Aislin asked still staring dumbly at the papers spread before her.

"Look at the dates." Irsa insisted, pulling out the contract for each and setting it beside the death certificate. "Each of them died a year before their contract was up."

Aislin shook her head. "She couldn't have been doing this all along; someone would have noticed. Right?"

"Maybe, I don't know. Otherwise, why would she have set up shop her of all places?" Irsa asked, realization dawning on her. This had been going on for decades, at least. "This is the exact contract I signed. There is no loophole; I can't just quit. I finish, or I die."

In, out — one deep inhale — Aislin nodded. "Right then, there is only one option left."

Irsa's heart stuttered at the thought. She had hurt no one on purpose before. "Won't it leave a mark," she asked softly.

"We don't have to kill her with anything violent, Irsa. We can poison her," Aislin reasoned.

"I meant on my magic. Won't killing someone, leave a mark on my magic?" That's what her mother had said to her. That death would taint her power.

Aislin reached for her hand, lifting it to brush a kiss to the back of it. "This is not the same as then," she whispered. "This won't be out of anger or for vengeance. It's self-preservation. And besides, we won't use your magic to do it. We'll brew a poison."

Irsa threaded her fingers through Aislin's, tightening her hold on the other girl. She drew strength from their connection, lifted her chin, and decided. "I have no other choice."

"No, Irsa, we have no other choice. We're in this together. Whatever mark it leaves, it'll leave it on both of us, I promise. You won't have to do this alone." Aislin vowed softly.

"Together," Irsa agreed.

"Good." Aislin moved to gather up the papers one-handed, refusing to drop Irsa's hand. "If you still have the book of poisons, go home and get it. We'll pick one out tonight, at my place, and I can gather the ingredients this week."

Irsa squeezed her friend's hand tighter, wearing on her lip. She could hardly believe they were even talking about murder, much less making a plan to do it. Worry twisted in her belly, making her ill. It was one thing to know she had no choice; it was another altogether to make the plan.

Aislin sensed her unease, and her freckled fingers stopped fiddling with the papers. She turned to Irsa, her free hand lifting to cup Irsa's cheek gently. "I won't let anything bad happen to you," she promised, and then kissed Irsa soft, but firmly on the lips.

The softness settled the racing of Irsa's heart, and the firmness calmed her belly. She was not alone. Aislin would be there right beside her to help her take care of this.

Chapter Eight

The ocean seemed small and quiet as Irsa laid with Aislin in her too-small bed, tails pressed together at the sides, flipping through the book of poisons and healing spells. All she could hear over the steady beating of her own heart was the slow fall of one seaweed page against the next. In the silence, the task ahead seemed that much graver.

"We need something quick, so she hasn't time to figure it out and make a cure," Aislin muttered pensively.

"But not too quick," Irsa argued. "If she drops dead suddenly, people will be suspicious. It needs to look like she's taken ill and then died from whatever it was." She had given this some thought, more than she would have liked honestly.

"If you insist," came an irritated grumble from Aislin, and she flipped the page away from the poison with the words 'instant death' under it. A few pages later she stopped, eyes squinting at the words on the page for a moment before asking, "What about this one? It says it mimics nettle sickness. I mean, she could have gotten that anywhere."

Irsa frowned, shaking her head. She knew exactly what nettle sickness did to the body. "I don't want her to suffer, Aislin."

"Why in Amphitrite's name not?" Aislin growled lowly, the sound surprising Irsa who jerked away from her friend—nearly toppling from the little bed. "She's been hurting you and murdered countless others. Had we not realized what she was doing, she would have killed you too and drained you of your power. She deserves to suffer for what she did."

Irsa squared her shoulders, her mouth thinning into a line. "Maybe that's so, but I cannot cause another being's suffering. Is it not enough that I will be the one to cause her death? Is that not enough harm?"

Freckled fingers latched onto Irsa's chin, meeting her eyes with a fury unlike any she had ever seen in Aislin's green depths before. "She hurt you. She deserves this," Aislin all but begged.

"She deserves it, yes," Irsa agreed softly, nodding. "But I don't."

With a heavy sigh, Aislin released her chin and nodded. "All right then, we'll pick something that won't make her suffer."

They chose a poison that would take a week to finish the job—according to the book. During that time, Calypso's health would seem to decline naturally, and eventually, she would die peacefully in her sleep. Amphitrite willing, she would not catch onto the fact that her apprentice was poisoning her before the week was out.

When Calypso returned at the end of the week, Irsa had a small store of the poison mixed and waiting for her. That evening, Irsa waited until Demeter had prepared Calypso's evening tray to strike.

"I think the Mistress wanted me to bring her, her tray," Irsa volunteered softly upon swimming into the kitchen.

With a shrug, Demeter moved. "Have at it, she's in a ripe mood," Demeter warned, then swam off.

Irsa took a quick look around the kitchen to ensure it was empty, then dumped the first dose of poison into the tea. Stirring compulsively, she hoped that Calypso wouldn't notice the color was a little lighter than usual. With a deep, calming breath she set the cup next to Calypso's evening snack—a kelp and jellyfish wrap—then balanced it on her hip. The door to Calypso's study was closed, so Irsa knocked softly.

"Enter," Calypso called from somewhere within. Her brows rose at the sight of Irsa swimming towards her with the tray. "What's this?"

"Your evening tray, Mistress," Irsa whispered with her head bowed low.

"Yes, I can see that," Calypso snapped. "Why in Poseidon's name are you carrying it? Where is Demeter?"

"I thought it best to let her get back to her other work as we will have guests soon." It wasn't technically a lie—in Irsa's mind—as they had guests coming in a fortnight, and Demeter did have a lot to attend to, which may have been why it left her lips so readily.

Blue eyes fixed Irsa with a suspicious glare for a long moment, all the while the tray became heavier and heavier in her hands. "Very well," Calypso muttered finally, gesturing to a space on the desk dismissively.

Irsa didn't wait to be told twice. She set the tray in the space, spun, and swam out of the room without another word. Once in the hall, she pressed her overheated back into the cold, rough coral wall, trying to catch her breath. "One down," she whispered to herself, squeezing her eyes shut and sending up a silent prayer to Amphitrite that the next day, it would be easier.

IT WAS, Calypso didn't even ask the following night when Irsa brought her evening tray. Nor the third or fourth. And by the fifth evening, Calypso slumped behind her desk, breathing heavily, barely able to keep her eyes open.

"Mistress, are you all right?" Irsa asked, setting the tray on the desk and swimming to Calypso's side. Long gray-brown fingers brushed a strand of black hair back from Calypso's hot forehead. "Oh Mistress, you're burning up. Let's get you into bed, shall we?"

"Y-yes, I think that might be best," Calypso agreed, weakly. She let Irsa help her out of her chair and lead her to the upper floors. When they reached Calypso's bedroom, Irsa helped her into it. Slim fingers tugged the seal lined blanket up over her. Irsa turned to go. Calypso grabbed her wrist to stop her. "Stay with me, won't you?"

Irsa swallowed, nodding. She settled onto the edge of her Mistress' soft mattress, holding her hand. "I'll be right here, all night, Mistress."

"Such a good girl," Calypso mumbled, her breathing becoming more labored. Her lids drooped, and she settled into a drugged sleep.

Irsa squeezed her eyes shut, willing her heart to beat more slowly, but it obstinately refused. Calypso would die. One more dose, maybe two, that would be the end. "Could that really be it?" Irsa asked herself.

She clenched Calypso's hand firmly, wondering if she could finish the thing she had started. It seemed too easy now that it was almost over. Calypso's grip loosened when she fell into a deeper sleep. The old witch looked almost sweet with her face relaxed, and her eyes closed. She looked nothing like the horrible person Irsa knew her to be.

"Please, Amphitrite," Irsa prayed softly. "Let her go tonight in her sleep. Let her know no pain and find peace." That was the best any of them could hope for, especially one who had made enemies through the years. Aislin was right. She was a foul creature who deserved this. But that did not make it easier.

For a while, it seemed she would go in her sleep. The old witch's breathing became shallower and shallower, barely disturbing the surrounding water. Peace, at last, Irsa could see it in her slumbering face. Irsa leaned in to brush a stray strand of hair back from her Mistress' face. Despite how horrible the woman had been to her, Irsa couldn't bring herself to hate Calypso. For many years she'd been a mother to Irsa. Still, she knew in the end, it would be Calypso's life or her own.

"Goodbye Mistress," Irsa whispered rising from her spot. Calypso would pass in the night whether or not she sat at her bedside. Besides, if she grew worse, it would look suspicious if Irsa didn't call for a doctor. It would be better if she weren't there at all.

Her reach for the door was pulled up short by a blood-curdling scream. Irsa whipped around, swimming quickly for the bed. Calypso's back arched off the bed, the wail continued on and on, seeming to never stop. Her eyes were wide open but had rolled back into her head. All color had drained from her skin.

"Sh. Sh. Sh. Quiet, Mistress," Irsa urged. Her fingers

brushing more hair back from Calypso's head, trying to soothe her. "It'll be all right, it'll all be over soon."

This didn't quiet the woman, her screaming continued, followed by violent thrashing and foaming at the mouth. In that moment, all thought left Irsa, she just acted. She only meant to muffle Calypso's shrieking when she grabbed the seal-down pillow to press over her Mistress' face. Calypso seemed to screech louder, her long red nails scraping at Irsa's skin. She fought to get away, to escape, to breathe! And the harder she fought, the harder Irsa had to press the pillow down to keep her silent.

She pressed harder and harder until eventually Calypso just stopped. Her screaming stopped. Her thrashing ceased. Her limbs no longer moved. Chest heaved with labored breath, pulling the pillow away, she found that Calypso had also ceased to breathe. The witch's face was entirely slack, her eyes open but unblinking, and no breath moved her chest.

"Calypso?" Irsa asked, unsure. She pressed a hand to the witch's chest and felt no movement from her heart. A moment later, light burst forth from where Irsa's hand pressed to Calypso's chest, and her power rushed back to her. It filled her with warmth and alertness—fleshing out her cheeks and bringing brightness back to her tail. It whispered *'freedom'* on the water.

Emotions washed over her like the tide.

First, disbelief. All this time, Irsa's power had been just out of reach. Now it was back. And Calypso—Calypso was dead. Was it all real? Or was this some dirty trick the witch was playing on her? Moments passed, during which Irsa's own breathing regulated.

Next came relief. It was over, and Irsa was free—finally. She could leave this village and move into the city with Aislin. There, she could open her own shop and make a reasonable living for herself. Happiness, it seemed, was in reach.

When relief dried up, revulsion settled in. "I-I killed her," Irsa sobbed, looking down at her hands—perhaps searching for some sign of blood. She found none, but that didn't stop her belly from rolling. The retching began shortly after, leaving behind a cloud of sick in the water.

She continued to retch until all that came up was bile. Swiping at her mouth with the back of her hand, she willed away the cloud of sick with her magic, squeezing her eyes shut.

With another deep breath, Irsa decided—the only one she had open to her, really. In the dead of night, Irsa packed her things and left it all behind her. She was free for the first time in years, and she would not wait around for that to change.

THE USUAL HOUR and a half swim into the village took half the time with the frantic energy coursing through Irsa's veins. She was at Aislin's door in no time, knocking lightly and praying to Amphitrite not to wake anyone else in the small building. When no answer came, she closed her eyes to reach for her magic and let it do the work. The door popped open a moment later, creaking quietly on its hinges, and she slipped inside.

Aislin was curled up on the tiny kelp-lined bed where they had lain together, plotting the murder of Calypso. Her green eyes were closed, and her lips slightly agape, face relaxed and at peace. Just as Calypso's had been in death. The memory crawled into Irsa's belly and made her dizzy with rage, grief, and uncertainty. They twisted in her gut, making her nauseous again and whimpered lowly, reaching for the bed to brace herself.

It dipped under her weight, waking Aislin from her sleep. Aislin blinked blearily at her friend. "Irsa?" She asked sleepily, then a moment later, "Are you all right? What time is it?"

"I—I don't know," Irsa rasped softly, her throat suddenly rough. She stared down at her hands in her lap, fingers twitching in agitation—still no blood.

Sitting up quickly, Aislin encircled her in freckled arms and tugged Irsa onto her lap to hold her close. "Tell me what happened," she insisted, her words low on the current, barely loud enough for Irsa to hear.

Irsa tried to tell her. She tried to say the words, 'she's dead, I killed her.' But all she managed was a tiny squeak before sobs wracked her body, and she pressed her face into Aislin's shoulder. They sat there for a long while, Aislin stroked her back soothingly, waiting for Irsa to cry herself out, and when she had, when there was nothing left, she took a deep breath and sat up. "We have to go now."

She wasn't sure what she had been expecting from Aislin—maybe she'd thought her friend would ask why, where, when—but all Aislin did was rise from the bed and pull a small packed bag from beneath it. "I have a carriage ready for us in the next town over; we must go on fin to get there, but after that we can go anywhere. We're free," Aislin assured her, kissing Irsa's cheek quickly.

Then she reached one freckled hand to pull Irsa to her fin, and the two escaped under the cover of darkness.

Chapter Nine

Starting over with Aislin—building a life with her—was easier, better than Irsa could have ever imagined.

A stark contrast to the villages where both girls had grown up, the city of Flottebo surrounded the castle of Alon—every winding street and shining window burned with the life of Alon's people. Even long into the night, Flottebo was a flurry of activity. It was easy for two girls—who wanted to go unnoticed—to get lost in the hustle and bustle of the place. To everyone around them, they were just two girls from a small village come to find their fortune.

It took them some time, but soon enough, they had found a small building in one of the poorer boroughs available to rent. It had two tiny shops on the main level, and an apartment above that was just large enough for the pair of them. They filled the space above with run down furniture they found on the side of the street, but somehow it was more like home than Irsa had known in years. Below, in one storefront, Irsa set up a small sea witch consulting business, and right next door was a tiny seamstress shop.

Over the coming year, they built themselves a small but happy life. Irsa helped anyone and everyone in their little corner of the world, making a name for herself as a kind and caring witch who sought to look after others while Aislin hemmed cloaks and patched tunics.

One day, as Aislin sat at her little drafting table in their apartment—sketching yet another beautiful gown that may never see the light of day—Irsa moved to lean over her shoulder, watching her. "We could move into a better part of the city," she murmured, thumb brushing over the bone in Aislin's shoulder. "You could make fancy dresses there."

"Then who would let out Jovana's frock when she becomes pregnant?" Aislin asked, lifting her head to smile at Irsa softly. "Besides, we can't afford another place yet; the rent is too good here. Maybe in a few years."

Irsa sighed, shaking her head. Sometimes she thought she was holding Aislin back—this was one of those times. "But these are so beautiful, they should be on someone," she insisted. "Maybe you could get work at bigger shops closer to the castle? Surely they need help."

"I have work here," Aislin said obstinately.

Irsa tugged Aislin's chin up gently to meet her eyes. "This is what you love; you should do this."

"Who will let out Jovana's frock?" Aislin insisted, her voice faltering just a little.

"You will. I'm not saying full time; I'm saying see if they need a part-time person to help. Get your fin in the door, show them your designs. Who knows what might happen. You deserve to see these come to life. I want you to try." Irsa's words left her in a rush. She wanted nothing more than to see Aislin doing what she'd always loved, to know the happiness Irsa knew.

Aislin's green eyes softened, and she nodded. "I'll try."

Not but a week later, Aislin rushed into Irsa's shop in a flurry of bubbles. "I've just been to see the seamstress who works just outside of the castle," she gushed.

Irsa lifted her head, raising an eyebrow in interest. "Yes?"

"You know sometimes she works for the prince when he's fed up with his father's stuffy old tailor?" Aislin continued, settling into the seat across from Irsa at her small table.

"No, I did not know that," Irsa responded patiently.

"Well, she does," Aislin insisted, teeth wearing on her full lower lip.

"That's exciting for them," Irsa drawled. "Now, are you through building the suspense?" Playful sarcasm dripped from every word, a smile tugging at the corner of Irsa's thin lips.

"Is it killing you?" Aislin asked, her eyes glittering in amusement.

"Absolutely."

Aislin giggled, floating higher and higher towards the ceiling—so close her head almost touched it. "They loved my work and want me to come in three times a week to create some original pieces for their clients." The words left her in a rush, followed by an ear-splitting squeal.

Irsa laughed, rising from the chair, to hug her friend tightly. "Oh Aislin, that's wonderful. You're going to take Alon's fashion scene by whirlpool," she whispered, hugging her friend more tightly.

"Everything is finally working out just how we wanted Irsa," Aislin murmured, kissing her happily.

Irsa squeezed her eyes shut, letting herself sink into the

kiss. It had been two years since Aislin had kissed her; she vowed to memorize it this time.

"Well, well, well," a voice echoed through the tiny shop, drawing the two merwomen away from each other. "So, this is where you've holed up, is it Irsa? You went from a manor, and luxury, to this." Disgust dripped from every word.

Irsa peered through the gloom of the early evening light until a mousy-haired, be-speckled mer came into view. "I expected more from Calypso's apprentice."

"Janette," Irsa asked, blinking in confusion.

"Hello, Irsa," Janette smirked, waving.

Irsa's stomach dropped to her fin, taking a deep breath. She lifted her chin. "What do you want, Janette?"

Janette's eyes flicked to Aislin, who was watching the pair of them with confusion. "I think we ought to have a chat. Privately, if you don't mind, dear?"

"I'm not going anywhere," Aislin frowned, rising from the chair to float behind Irsa.

"It's all right, Aislin, head home. I'll see you there." Irsa murmured, nodding when Aislin shot her a questioning look. Red hair flowing behind her, Aislin left the pair alone. "Okay Janette, what do you want?"

"You should have known better than to hide from the Council. It only makes you look guilty," Janette said casually, swimming over to the chair Aislin had just vacated and dropping into it.

"Are you here to make vague threats, or was there a legitimate purpose?" Irsa asked in annoyance, settling into the chair across from Janette.

The smirk on Janette's face tightened but didn't falter. "I'm here about your inheritance."

"My what?" Irsa asked, brows lifting.

"As an apprentice to a recently deceased sea witch, you

were left certain things. Her library, for one, but also her client list and some of her assets. Those assets were split between you and the Council, but there is still a hefty sum left for you, of course." Janette's eyes swept the tiny shop. "I'm sure you can make use of it—somehow."

Rolling her eyes, Irsa shook her head. "I want nothing left by Calypso. I'm just fine on my own."

"Well, that's too bad. Council law dictates you are to inherit these things. What you do with them once they're in your possession is of no concern of ours, but they will be delivered to you." Janette pulled out a rolled-up bit of seaweed scroll. "Here is a list of everything you'll be receiving. The books should arrive in about a fortnight, and we can deliver your monetary assets to you however you choose. Just fill out the form attached."

Irsa swallowed a snarl, taking the scroll. "Is that all?"

Janette smiled thinly, rising from her chair. "No, that is not all. The death of an elder is serious; upon your disappearance, the Council had no choice but to launch a formal investigation with the royal court."

Irsa fought to keep her face impassive, swallowing roughly. "Of course."

"I'll have more information for you soon on this." Janette headed for the door but stopped just before it to look at Irsa over her shoulder. "A word of advice, old friend, keep your head down lest you lose it, and don't go running into hiding again—it won't do you any good in the long run." Then she swam back out to her waiting carriage and was gone.

CURLED UP TOGETHER on the seagrass sofa that evening, Irsa took time to examine the list of books more closely.

"I just can't believe they hunted you down like a seal," Aislin was muttering. "Did she say when the investigation would start?" Aislin asked, her fingers working nervous knots into the end of her long red braid.

Irsa inhaled deeply, looking over at her friend to drink in the worried expression. She was worried too, but it would do them no good to be anxious about this. Whatever happened, happened. "No, she didn't. Let's try not to think about it. I'm sure it's just a formality," she reassured, gently pulling Aislin's hands out of the mangled hair to squeeze them with her own. "Be calm."

"All right," Aislin whispered, leaning in closer to snuggle beneath the thin kelp blanket.

Black eyes returned to the scroll before her as Irsa looked over the list. "Calypso's library was much larger than I ever knew," she muttered thoughtfully.

"Hm?" Aislin asked her gaze flicking down to the list as she leaned on Irsa's shoulder for a better look.

"And some of these books—" Irsa trailed off, shaking her head. "I can't believe the Council let her keep them, much less handed them off to me." Something felt wrong about it. The Council had every reason not to trust her, and they were giving her a collection of dangerous books? No, it wasn't right.

"Why? What's wrong with them?" Aislin narrowed her eyes on the list, trying to understand what about the titles seemed wrong.

"She has a whole collection—small as it might be—of books on dark magic. Stuff the Council wouldn't let her practice, so I don't know why they'd let her have them." Irsa pointed to one book, in particular, her nose wrinkling. "This? This is a book of plagues. You could take out all of Alon with this. Or a whole species of fish if you wanted to. There is no use for it other than to hurt people. Which isn't what sea witches are supposed to do."

Aislin frowned, turning to look up at Irsa from her shoulder. "Then don't use them?"

Irsa heaved a sigh and shook her head. "It's not that simple, Aislin. Just having them in the same place as my other books is dangerous. The magic living inside of them could corrupt even the most innocuous of spell books. I have to be very careful. And then there is the discussion of why they're letting me have them, which seems strange."

"Do you think they're testing you?" Worry threaded Aislin's words.

"If they are, this isn't the most covert way to do it," Irsa snorted. "They could be setting me up, though."

"What should we do?"

We. The word settled warmly into Irsa's heart, and she smiled gently. They were in this together. "For now, we wait and see what their plan is. I'll deal with these when they come in. In the meantime, you have to be at the shop in Fixa early tomorrow morning so we should get to bed."

Aislin looked at her for a long moment, worry still etched on her features, then nodded and rose from the sofa. Irsa allowed the list one more passing glance before folding up the blanket to replace on the back of the couch and heading to bed herself.

THE FIRST CRATE of books arrived not but three days later. Irsa pulled the books from it one by one, scrutinizing each. They were nothing special, mostly healing magic—full of spells Irsa had learned years ago. For a moment she considered not shelving them at all, but what was a sea witch without a library?

So, they joined her small collection of books on the shelves, one by one until she reached the bottom. There, at the very bottom of the crate was a thin scaly black volume with no title scrawled onto the cover.

She grabbed the book, her skin itched everywhere she brushed the scales. "You're an evil little piece of kit, aren't you?" She asked it softly. It rustled its pages in response. "We will have to put you somewhere safe." Irsa swam up high to tuck the book up into the top corner of a driftwood shelf right below the ceiling. "There, that ought to keep you out of the wrong hands until I can sort out what to do with you."

"I think you'll need more shelves soon," Aislin said from the door. "You'll have a proper witch's library in no time."

"I don't know that I'll keep them." Isa shrugged, sinking back down to the sand.

Aislin settled beside her and asked, "Why not?"

Irsa sighed, leaning into Aislin lightly. "After everything that happened, I don't know that I want any part of her here. This is our place, and she doesn't belong here." There was a wrongness that had settled into Irsa's belly the moment she'd opened that crate; she couldn't explain it. It was as if the books themselves knew what she'd done to her mistress, and they were judging her for it.

A freckled hand settled onto her forearm, giving it a gentle squeeze. "Irsa, you were her apprentice. This is your right. But if they don't make you comfortable, then we can get rid of them."

With a deep breath, Irsa nodded. Aislin was right, Calypso's library was hers by right, but that didn't make the wrongness go away. "Perhaps I'll keep them just until I can build up my own library?"

"That sounds like an excellent plan to me." Aislin

tugged Irsa in close to give her a tight hug. "In the meantime, let's get lunch."

CRATES OF BOOKS continued to arrive every day for a fortnight until Irsa's small shop was full, from floor to ceiling with her Mistress' library. She carefully tucked the last of the dark magic books up with the others, ignoring the way they made her skin crawl to touch them. "Out of sight and out of mind until I can come up with a way to dispose of you," she whispered to them softly. They seemed to whisper back in agitation, pages fluttering but didn't move to stop her.

The bell chimed lightly over the door, and Irsa turned to see Janette swimming through the door. "Do you really think quarantining them will be enough?" She asked, quirking one brow.

"Enough for what?" Irsa countered, her arms crossing over her chest.

"To save your tail, old friend."

"I don't know what you're talking about," Irsa responded, moving to the small table in the center of the room littered with papers. "Now, if you'll excuse me, I have work to do. There is a merwoman two streets over in desperate need of a morning sickness draught."

"You can't just make this go away by keeping your head low and performing meaningless healing magic." Janette sat across from Irsa. "They will know."

"Know what, Janette?"

"If you performed any dark magic, it will have left a mark. They'll test you; they'll see it. You can't hide from this," Janette insisted.

"Well, if they plan to investigate me then I'd suggest

they get it over with so, we can all get on with our lives. Don't you think?" Irsa asked brazenly.

Janette sat, flabbergasted, her mouth moving open and closed like a fish for a long moment. Then she seemed to compose herself and rose from the chair. "I'll be seeing you Irsa."

"Yes, I suppose you will. Have a nice evening, Janette." Janette turned in the water, swimming away quickly, leaving Irsa to her papers.

A moment later, the bell chimed again, this time Aislin swam in. "What was that about?"

"Nothing to worry about. Let's go home for supper, shall we?" Irsa asked, collecting the papers she needed for the spell and heading to the door. "I'm hungry."

Aislin looked at her suspiciously but said no more. All Irsa could hope was that the Council was making empty threats, and they would leave her alone now.

Chapter Ten

Free from thinly veiled threats and visits from Janette or any other Council members, Irsa helped Jovana, and many others in their borough deliver happy, healthy children. Aislin's designs began to gain recognition amongst the elite circles of Alon. Their life was a quiet, peaceful one for nearly a year.

Irsa had relaxed into their routine. She swam to the door of her shop, flipping the sign that read 'out to lunch', and swam over to Aislin's for their regular lunch date — twice a week, no matter how busy they were. Aislin was waiting at the small table in the back room of her shop; their lunch spread out before her. "You're late," she chided playfully.

"I know, Gwenifer was in for her weekly treatment. Who knew Calypso's collection of fertility spells would be so useful," Irsa murmured, settling at the table across from her friend.

Full lips twitched in sympathy, and Aislin nodded. "How is she? Is it working?"

Irsa felt the weight of the question sink onto her shoulders. It was always hard to help these women—even harder when it didn't seem that her help was working. "Honestly, I don't know yet. It's still too early to tell if the pregnancy has taken or not. All we can do is hope and pray for the best."

"I'll make another offering to Amphitrite in the morning," Aislin offered solemnly.

A soft smile stretched Irsa's face. She reached over to take her friend's hand, giving it a gentle squeeze. The pair settled into a comfortable silence after that, enjoying one another's company, and the food spread before them. The sharp sound of a knock on the shop next door interrupted the peace. "It might be a client," Irsa mumbled, moving to rise.

"If it is, they can wait. You'll only be gone a little longer; I'm sure it's not that important. Sit," Aislin urged.

"What if it's an emergency?" Irsa's fingers twisted nervously.

"Then they know they can come here. Just relax," Aislin soothed.

Irsa settled into the seat again, letting Aislin's words calm her a little. But then another knock followed persistently. "Irsa of Tjena, I am Gavril, and I am here on official business from the Council of Alon," a male voice yelled at the door.

Irsa rose quickly, swimming to the door before Aislin could stop her, and peaked out at the well-muscled merman standing before her shop. "What can I help you with, Gavril?"

"I have been instructed to search your shop for remnants of dark magic," he informed her, floating up a little straighter and lifting his chin so he could look his down his long nose at her with amber-colored eyes.

"And do you have any official paperwork from the Council about this?" Aislin asked, appearing suddenly at her side.

"It's all right, Aislin; I have nothing to hide," Irsa assured. She swam over to her shop, opened the door for Gavril and let him inside. "Has the Council said what this is about?"

Instead of answering, Gavril pulled a scroll from his tunic pocket and began to take rapid-fire notes. It didn't take long for him to find the small cache of black magic books tucked away at the back of the shop. "What of these?" He asked.

"What of them? They were willed to me, with all the others from my previous Mistress," Irsa answered.

"And you have put them to good use?" He inquired, jotting down something on the parchment.

Irsa quirked a brow at the leading question but answered smoothly. "No, I have quarantined them from all the other books and ignored them. I have no use for dark magic and don't intend to have any use for it." It wasn't a lie, she had only ever used dark magic once, and she never intended to use it again.

"Are you telling me that those books haven't been touched since you received them?" Gavril asked, accusation dripping from every word, sharp amber eyes narrowing on her.

"I placed them on the shelf, that was it."

"Very well then, you won't mind if we send someone to inspect them, and prove that will you?"

"Not at all. I look forward to getting this cleared up," Irsa smiled tightly. "Until then, I was having lunch with my friend, and then I have clients to see. So, I trust you can see yourself out?"

Gavril looked at her for a long moment, irritation etched in his features, but he said nothing more. When he left Irsa slumped forwards, taking a heavy gulp of sea water to calm her frazzled nerves.

"When will they be back?" Aislin asked, swimming over to take Irsa's hands.

"I don't know. But if they're starting with the books, then that gives us a bit of time to think before they test me personally." Aislin nodded slowly.

"We'll think of something before then."

It seemed the Council was busy with other matters for the time being because they left Irsa to her quiet life for a full month. During that time, little changed aside from Aislin's designs grew even more in notoriety. Then one day, as Irsa came home from the market, she found the royal carriage parked outside of Aislin's little shop.

Swimming closer, Irsa peeked inside and frowned. A handsome, square-jawed, electric blue-haired young man she recognized immediately as Prince Tynan, floated just before Aislin, chest puffed out in pride like an overgrown sea lion. Irsa entered before she realized there was even a choice to make.

"Irsa," Aislin yelped excitedly, her eyes wide, and smile bright. "May I introduce you to—"

"Prince Tynan, son of King Hemnes, and heir to the throne of Alon," Tynan cut her off, falling into a regal bow that Irsa was sure was well-practiced to charm the scales off any mer he met. "And you are?" He reached for her hand, smiling roguishly up at her.

What Irsa wanted to say was, 'of course, you are.' What she said was, "Irsa of Tjena. A pleasure, I'm sure."

"A pleasure, indeed," he announced before bending his head to kiss the back of her hand. The gesture sent an unpleasant shiver up her spine, as did the way his bright eyes met hers. Aislin twittered amused from where she floated nearby.

"Right," Irsa muttered awkwardly, pulling her hand away from his grasp. She resisted the urge to rub it on her cloak. "I thought I'd bring you lunch on my way up to the apartment." She reached into the bag to pull out a wrap carefully covered in cloth.

"Ooh, thank you! I'm starved," Aislin giggled, kissing Irsa's cheek and taking the little wrap from her. "I'm going to finish up measuring the prince for his new tunic; then I'll be done for the day. Are we still on for dinner?"

"Of course." Irsa nodded. "I'll see you soon." She spun to head up to their tiny apartment. The water grew dark and cold as time wore on, all the while, Irsa watched shadows dance across the light of the shop below. It was well passed dinner time when Aislin floated in on a cloud of giggles. Irsa swallowed down the jealousy to give her friend a stern but playful look. "That was quite some fitting."

"Well, he's quite some prince, is he not?" Aislin flopped down onto the couch, smiling at her friend. "Come now, Irsa, don't be cross. It was one dinner."

"With a very handsome prince," Irsa grumbled, crossing her arms over her chest. She felt petulant and silly, but if anyone knew Aislin's flights of fancy, it was Irsa.

"Who is ordering a new tunic, and then he'll be gone from our lives forever. Nothing to worry about at all," Aislin assured her, arms wrapping around her friend and squeezing her tightly. "You have nothing to be jealous of."

"I'm not jealous," Irsa protested, but even to her, it sounded weak.

"No, of course not," Aislin agreed. She pressed a kiss to

Irsa's cheek and sighed gently. "Besides, it would be good for us to have friends in high places."

Irsa was too tired to ask what Aislin meant by that, so she stayed silent, curling into the warmth of her friend and wishing away the world outside their small apartment. Full of princes, and the Council, and clients. For a moment, she wanted nothing more than to be with Aislin.

Gavril returned with a witch with long flowing orange hair. "Irsa of Tjena, we are here to inspect your stock of black magic books," the witch insisted softly.

Irsa nodded, letting them into the shop without a fight. What point was there in fighting it? It only would have made her look guilty. "As I told you before, those books haven't been touched since I shelved them a year ago," Irsa insisted. "This really is a waste of everyone's time."

"We'll be the judge whether or not it's a waste of time." Gavril growled, amber eyes narrowing on her.

Irsa wasn't sure what she'd done to make the man so angry, but she shrugged it off. Now wasn't the time to make enemies. She showed them where the books were and floated back to let them do their work. The orange-haired witch—who went by Divna—pulled each book from the shelf, scrutinizing it. Then she ran one pudgy finger down its spine, and the book spat out a puff of black ink. When that was done, Gavril and Divna muttered to each other in hushed tones before turning back to Irsa. "You have not used any of these books," Divna said stiffly.

"Just as I said," Irsa answered, her eye twitching with annoyance. "Will that be all?"

"For now," Gavril grunted. Irsa allowed the pair to see themselves out, sinking into a chair with a huff. For now, she was safe. How much longer her luck would win out, she didn't know.

"I HAVE GOOD NEWS, and I have better news," Aislin announced a fortnight later. "Which would you like first?" The basket of groceries thunked onto their small kitchen table.

"You're awfully chipper for someone who hasn't slept in two days," Irsa muttered irritably, her head still reeling from a night of night terrors involving an angry man with amber eyes.

"I said, which would you like first?" Aislin repeated her eyes narrowing on her friend. When Irsa gave no sign that she'd answer, Aislin forged onward. "There is to be a royal ball in two months."

"So, which one was that? The good news or the better news?" Irsa asked a little smirk twitching her lips in teasing.

"You really are impossible, Irsa," Aislin huffed, flopping onto a chair.

"You love it." Irsa's smirk widened.

"That's besides the point."

"I think it's the whole point," Irsa argued, reaching out to brush her fingers down the length of Aislin's arm. "Come on, tell me the better news."

"No, you're just going to make fun," Aislin responded petulantly.

"I won't, I promise."

Aislin uncrossed her arms, beaming again. "Tynan has commissioned me to make him something spectacular for the event!"

Irsa swallowed down the slithering green tentacle of

jealousy and forced a smile. "That's fantastic news, Aislin! I'm sure it'll be the most splendid thing he's ever worn!" She rose to hug her friend tightly, squeezing her eyes shut to force away the dread that floated on the tide.

"He said the exact same thing," Aislin giggled girlishly.

'Of course, he did,' Irsa thought.

Chapter Eleven

In a whirl of fittings and fabric choices—all of which put Aislin and Prince Handsomer-than-an-angelfish in annoyingly close proximity—the ball drew closer. Every day was a struggle with the jealous monster threatening to take over every inch of her being. But somehow, she managed it. It was just clothes; she told herself, nothing more.

Aislin poured herself into bed late one evening, her fingers red and sore from sewing. "Will you use that healing spell on them?" She begged softly.

"Of course," Irsa swam to her bedside. With a murmur, her magic swirled in the water, weaving in and out of Aislin's stretched fingers until they were no longer red. "All better," she smiled gently, lifting one of Aislin's hands to her lips to brush a kiss to her fingertips.

"Thank you," Aislin sighed, sinking further into the soft kelp mattress.

"Are you finished the prince's ridiculous frock yet?" Irsa asked, settling onto the bed next to her friend, brushing tendrils of red hair back from her face. "You need a rest."

"Nearly. He has his last fitting tomorrow." Aislin twined her fingers with Irsa's squeezing them. "And then, you and I, my friend, will have enough money to leave Alon behind us."

Irsa blinked for a moment, unsure that she'd heard correctly. "Leave Alon? Why?"

"To protect you," Aislin answered. "I don't know what the Council will do with you if they find out you've used dark magic. And even if they don't, I don't think they'll stop until they've found a way to pin Calypso's murder on you. The safest thing to do is leave."

Leave—it had never seemed like much of an option to Irsa. Although she had no ties to Alon, Aislin still had family here. Alon was home. "What about your family? And your business! What about the life we've built here?"

Inhaling deeply, Aislin sat up, her freckled fingers reaching out to cup Irsa's cheek. "There is no life here without you in it. So if we have to leave to keep you safe, then we will. We'll move to another kingdom and start over."

"I don't want you to make that sacrifice for me," Irsa protested.

"Well, good thing I'm not asking you." Aislin shook her head, smiling ruefully.

"There has to be another option. What about your prince? What will he say?"

"He's not my prince," Aislin laughed, flopping back onto the bed. "He won't marry some commoner." A sad smile stretched her lips.

"Do you love him?" Irsa asked her chest clenching.

"I think I'm beginning to," Aislin answered, closing her eyes.

Did it hurt? Yes, but Aislin had dreamed of a prince sweeping her off her fin all of her life. So, of course, she would fall for the too-handsome prince. He was the dream. "Then we'll stay and see what happens," Irsa declared. "Maybe they won't find anything, and they'll leave me alone. If they don't, we'll come up with another solution."

Aislin looked up at her, frowning, and shook her head. "If they find something, this is the solution. That is it."

And she would speak no more on the topic.

TYNAN ARRIVED for his final fitting the following day. He swept into the little shop as if he owned the place, glaring at Aislin's other client until they left, and paying Irsa no mind.

"Miss Aislin, beautiful as ever," he purred, bowing low in greeting before Aislin, who just giggled in response. "I hope I haven't come too early. I know my fitting was scheduled for this evening, but I could not wait to see you again." A charming, flirtatious smile split his lips. It was met with more giddy giggles from Aislin.

Irsa rose from her seat, fully intent on excusing herself. "I'll see you for dinner, Aislin," she muttered, swimming for the door.

"You don't have to," Aislin protested, her eyes flicking to her friend.

"It's all right; I have clients waiting," she kissed Aislin's cheek and swam out the door. *'This was for the best,'* she told herself. Aislin deserved happiness, and the puffed-up pufferfish of a prince was her best chance at that. She tried not to sulk as she flopped into the chair behind her tiny desk to work.

HOURS TICKED BY, and eventually, Irsa closed up shop to

head home. One glance at the seamstress shop next door told her that the prince was still there with Aislin. It was well into the night before Aislin returned to their small apartment above. Her face was flushed, and her eyes were bright with excitement.

"What now?" Irsa asked, rubbing at the bridge of her nose. "Don't tell me he proposed or something equally ridiculous."

"No. Better," Aislin giggled, practically vibrating with her excitement.

"Better? What's better than a proposal from a prince?" Confusion creased Irsa's brow.

"He invited me to the ball!" Aislin's words burst from her loudly. "The ball! Me! Oh, Irsa, can you imagine?"

Irsa shook her head, smiling softly. "You'll need a dress then, I suppose."

"A dress! Oh, great Poseidon, I don't have any kind of time to make myself a dress!" Aislin exclaimed, her hands moving to twist in the length of braid pulled over her shoulder.

Rising from her bed, Irsa swam to her friend, pulling her hands from her red hair. "You leave that to me, Aislin. I'll find you the perfect thing to wear. Focus on finishing the prince's clothes, and all your other work, and I'll take care of dressing you."

Aislin squealed, throwing her arms around Irsa to hug her tightly. "I love you," she whispered, kissing her friend's cheek.

IRSA HAD NEVER MADE CLOTHING, but she knew what Aislin would look best in, so she worked from that. After digging through Calypso's library of basic home magic, she found a book full of sewing spells. While Aislin worked away at garments for others, Irsa created an emerald green gown to match her tail.

The night before the ball, it was finally finished. Irsa took her time, laying it out on the sofa in their small living area. Then she settled into a chair to read. She had just begun to doze when a sudden gasp woke her.

"Oh Irsa, it's perfect," Aislin breathed, her fingers trembling when she reached for the silky fabric.

"Try it on," Irsa said, scrubbing at her face tiredly.

"W-what?"

"Try it on, silly. I didn't make it for you to just look at it," Irsa snorted, rising from the chair.

"Will it fit?" Aislin lifted the gown, holding it up to herself to check. "It looks like it may be a bit too big," she commented, doing a quick twirl.

"Trust me, just go put it on," Irsa motioned to the screen in their bedroom. Aislin nodded, draping the gown over her arm, and swimming to the screen to duck behind it.

A few minutes later, she gasped loudly. "It's magic!"

Irsa chuckled softly. "Yes, it's magic. Now come out. Let's see it."

"You could make a business of this, completely cut out the need for a seamstress," Aislin babbled, moving from behind the screen to do a little twirl for Irsa. "It fits perfectly."

Irsa watched Aislin, her heart hammering in her chest. She was beautiful, magnetic, there was no way anyone at the ball could ignore her in that dress. Irsa swallowed roughly and wondered for a moment if she'd just signed away her dear Aislin for forever.

"It's perfect Irsa. Thank you." Aislin swam to her, hugging her tightly. "I wish you could come with me. We'd have so much fun."

Irsa wished that too if just to look after her friend. "No, it's all right. You have fun. Dance with your prince." She kissed Aislin's cheek and pulled back with a soft smile.

"W ILL you braid my hair like you used to?" Aislin asked, looking at Irsa in the mirror. They had decided not to open their respective shops that day and instead focus on getting Aislin ready for the ball.

"If that's how you want to wear it." Irsa's fingers twisted in Aislin's long red hair, smoothing it slowly. Aislin nodded, grinning at her friend, and Irsa began to work her magic, weaving the red tresses into an intricate crown braid atop Aislin's head. Her magic began to glitter at the tips of her fingers, leaving glittering stars in its wake. "Beautiful," she smiled gently at Aislin.

Aislin opened her mouth to respond but was stopped by a demanding knock at their front door. The two merwomen stilled, looking at the door in confusion. "It's too early for the carriage," Aislin whispered.

"I'll get it, it could be an emergency." Irsa turned and swam to the door. Floating on the other side was Gavril and two angry-looking guards. "Is there something we can help you with?" Irsa asked, quirking a brow.

"Irsa of Tjena, you are under arrest." Gavril growled right before the guard moved to grab her arm and clamp shackles on her wrist.

"Excuse me? Let me go!" Irsa growled tugging away from the man. "I've done nothing wrong!"

"What's the meaning of this?" Aislin asked, rushing over to them. "What's the charge?"

"The Council has deemed you a flight risk," Gavril answered, a victorious smile splitting his lips. "They ordered that you be held in the dungeons until your trial in a fortnight."

"You can't do that," Aislin growled, grabbing one of Irsa's arms to tug her back into the apartment. "She hasn't done anything wrong!"

"I guess we'll see about that." Gavril smirked, yanking Irsa out of the apartment again.

"I'm not letting you take her." Aislin swam to float in front of them, her arms crossed.

"We've got an extra set of cuffs if you'd like to come with her." Gavril was guffawing at his own joke, his face lit in a cruel smirk.

Aislin opened her mouth to speak up again, but Irsa shook her head to silence her. "No Aislin, it's all right. Go to the ball. I'll see you soon."

"But—"

"It's all right. I'll be fine. A night in the dungeons won't hurt me, and in the morning we can talk about how to handle this. Just try to have fun?" Irsa urged her as best she could with shackled wrists. Aislin nodded, her hands twisting in the fabric of her gown as the guards dragged Irsa through the water to a barred carriage.

The carriage rocked, and Aislin grew smaller and smaller through the barred windows. When Irsa could no longer see her, she sighed and slunk down to the floor. It didn't take long for them to reach the dungeons once they had the guards dragged her from the carriage and tossed her into a cell.

"Can I at least get some supper?" Irsa called, but the bulky merman swam away without a word. "Right... no supper then." With a grunt, Irsa settled onto the hard bench, looking out the window at the streets of the city outside. Seahorses glittered in the jellyfish streetlights, attached to gilded carriages that trundled along the sand towards the main entrance of the castle. "The guests are arriving," she mumbled blandly. "I hope Aislin has fun, at least."

Irsa shut her eyes, curling tightly under the thin blanket they had provided her. She allowed the muffled music and chatter of the ball to lull her into a sleep full of dancing figures and sparkling gowns. A smile settling onto her face as her dreams turned to Aislin, flouncing about in the emerald green gown, her green eyes sparkling.

The slam of a door jerked her awake, but Irsa remained where she was, eyes still closed. "Your highness, I really don't think this wise. The Council has deemed her to be dangerous," a man was saying.

"Relax, Sebastian, I can handle this," Tynan's voice floated on the water.

"They say she's too powerful," Sebastian whispered earnestly. The words nearly tugged a smirk to Irsa's lips—too powerful.

"More reason to make peace with her," Tynan answered, his voice growing louder as they approached the cell. "Irsa of Tjena," he called softly. "Sebastian, give me the keys."

"But, You Highness, the Council—" Sebastian warned.

"The Council is still under my rule, and answers to me. As do you—now, open the damn door," Tynan growled finally, his voice carrying the power and authority of the Prince of Alon. Irsa heard the merman's hands shake as he jingled the key in the lock, and then the door opened with a slam. The water shifted as the prince swam towards her. "Irsa of Tjena," he murmured softly, reaching down to press a hand to her shoulder.

Irsa forced a heavy blink, her eyes opening and closing drowsily, as if she'd just woken from a deep sleep. "Prince

Tynan?" She asked, dragging her words to make herself sound sleepy. "What are you doing here?"

"I've come to release you," he straightened up, tilting his chin up a little like the hero of one of Aislin's ridiculous novels. "Gather yourself, Sebastian will see that you make it home safely."

"I will?" Sebastian asked, jerking as if he'd just been stricken.

"Yes, you will," Tynan answered his brilliant turquoise eyes cutting to Sebastian in warning. The red-haired merman gulped visibly and nodded, putting up no more protests. "Good, now, gather your things."

Irsa rose from the bench, her eyes wide. "Won't this upset the Council? Why are you doing this?"

Tynan shrugged. "Likely, but in the end, they answer to me not the other way around." There was a note of snobby pride that made Irsa want to punch Tynan, but she bit back the impulse. "Your friend Aislin asked me to. She promised me you were not a flight risk, and we could trust you. Can we trust you?"

With a deep breath, Irsa nodded. If Aislin had promised they wouldn't leave Alon, then they wouldn't leave Alon. Irsa would not turn her friend into a liar. "You can, Your Highness."

"Then you may return home, and await your trial there," Tynan nodded. "Sebastian?"

"Yes, Your Highness, the carriage is already out front. This way Lady Irsa," Sebastian gestured to the cell door, bent low at the waist. Irsa followed him out of the cell and then through the castle to the awaiting carriage.

"You don't have to come with me," Irsa offered softly once she had settled into the carriage. "I can make it home just fine."

"I'm sure you can," Sebastian grumbled blandly. His

hair may have been almost the same shade as Aislin's, but those eyes were nothing like her's, irises of amber narrowed on her in suspicion. She'd seen that gaze too frequently of late, she realized. "But the prince ordered that I accompany you, so I am." He settled onto the bench beside her in the carriage, rapping lightly on the roof spurring the driver into action.

They rode on in silence for a while, Irsa watching out of the window as the city rolled past them. Until she finally asked, "Did Aislin at least look like she was having a good time?"

Sebastian blinked at her for a moment, his brows narrowing. "Your little red-haired friend?" Irsa nodded. "The prince was showing her a dangerous amount of attention."

A frown twisted her features, and she looked back out the window. "A dangerous amount?"

"He has danced nearly every dance with her, bordering on shunning the other ladies," Sebastian informed her in a tone of distaste. "She's just something shiny, his infatuation will wear thin soon." Irsa wondered if he'd said it to soothe himself or her. Probably himself.

She said no more, letting the silence stretch between them as the carriage moved towards their shop. "Thank you," Irsa murmured, slipping from the carriage. Without a word, the driver and Sebastian headed back to the castle, leaving her in a flurry of bubbles. "Rude," she muttered.

Their small apartment was empty and silent in a way it had never been before—even when Aislin had been working late at the shop. She wrapped a blanket around herself to ward off the chill of the water and curled up on their kelp sofa, which was much too large without Aislin beside her.

She was still sitting there in the dark when Aislin

flopped through the door early the next day, slamming it behind her. The sound jerking her awake, Irsa glared at her friend, tugging the blanket further up on her neck. Aislin paid her no mind, throwing herself onto the couch beside her friend. Unsure of where to start, Irsa remained silent for a moment before saying, "I suppose I ought to thank you."

Aislin shrugged, leaning into Irsa and yawning. "No need," she muttered.

"Did you have fun at least while you were out there saving my tail?" Irsa looped her arms around her friend, hugging her close.

"The prince is quite the dancer," was Aislin's only answer, a little giggle escaping her.

"And very charming, I'm sure," Irsa murmured, pressing her nose into Aislin's still braided hair with a sigh.

"Oh, exceedingly charming." Aislin nodded with another giggle. "Nothing on you though," she teased softly.

"No, of course not." Irsa smiled softly, and they fell into silence for a moment. Irsa let her mind wander, thinking of everything that had happened in such a short amount of time. Then she asked, "So we're staying in Alon?"

Aislin nodded with a soft sigh. "For now, at least, we are staying in Alon. Until your name is cleared."

Dark eyes pinching shut, Irsa exhaled deeply and nodded. "That was probably our best course of action, anyway."

Chapter Twelve

"You should have been there Irsa. There was so much delicious food to eat, and everyone was dressed in all their finest. You would have loved it," Aislin said with stars in her eyes still a week later, spinning in a circle at the center of Irsa's shop. She had regaled Irsa with every tiny detail from the ball for the last week. Still it seemed to be the only thing she could talk of.

Jealousy flared up inside her, but Irsa swallowed it down. "I'm glad you enjoyed yourself," she whispered in return. There was a part of her that wondered if now that Aislin had had a taste of that life would she ever be satisfied with their simple life again? But she didn't ask it out loud for fear of what the answer would be.

"I'm sorry, am I boring you? I can't seem to help it," Aislin giggled.

"Not at all, I enjoy seeing you so happy." Irsa smiled softly, that at least was not a lie. "Will you be seeing the prince again, do you think?"

"Oh, I don't think so. The king seemed adamant that

Tynan ought to court the princess from Jonaxel." Aislin shrugged, her tone unhindered by sadness or regret.

"But what about you?" Irsa frowned, swimming over to where her friend floated. "I thought you were in love with him?"

Aislin smiled softly, her fingers brushing over Irsa's cheek. "I suppose I could have been; he is handsome. But there is more to life than being handsome."

Irsa nodded, smiling softly. "I guess there is." Still, she worried that, if given the chance, Aislin would choose that life of delicious food and shimmering parties over their simple life.

THE FOLLOWING DAY, as the pair settled in for their regular lunch routine, Irsa received her answer.

The 'out to lunch' sign had been turned on the door, that didn't seem to stop Prince Tynan, who knocked loudly at the door. When he received no answer, he used what little magic he had to unlock the door and barge right in. "Aislin of Tjena, I must speak with you," he called from where he floated just inside the front door.

Aislin and Irsa both peeked out from the backroom, brows raised. "Your Highness?" Aislin asked in confusion. "Is there something wrong?"

"No," he blurted, paused for a moment—breathing—and continued. "Yes. There is something wrong." Time seemed to stop as he fell to bent fin on the soft seagrass rug. "Aislin of Tjena, will you do me the honor of being my wife?"

Aislin blinked for a long moment, her green eyes wide with surprise. She looked over at Irsa thoughtfully before looking back to the prince. Her teeth wore on her full lip for another long moment before she shook her head.

"What was that?" Tynan asked, frowning at her in confusion.

"No, I will not marry you, Tynan," Aislin answered softly.

He jerked as if she'd stuck him, his turquoise brows creasing in annoyance. "I'm sorry?" Tynan asked as if he perhaps hadn't heard her correctly.

Aislin floated up a little straighter, lifting her chin, before saying, "I will not marry you, Tynan." Irsa felt her heart leap into her throat, her mind reeling in disbelief. Surely, Aislin hadn't just turned down the future king of Alon? Except, she had—twice now. "Now, if you'll excuse us, we were sitting down to lunch."

Aislin spun on her fin and returned to their small table in the backroom. Irsa watched the prince as he shook himself in confusion, much like her own. His face hardened, he turned on his fin and left, slamming the door behind him. Irsa went back to lunch, still puzzled over the events that had occurred. She badly wanted to ask Aislin, 'why,' but decided that perhaps it was best she didn't the answer.

Tynan returned twice more to ask again. Each time he grew more agitated with Aislin's continued rejection. On the last time, he came bearing a ridiculously large pearl ring.

"Aislin of Tjena," he begged, not bothering to get down on bent fin this time. "Make me the happiest man in all the sea and be my queen?"

Aislin sighed, scrubbing at her face, her eyes squeezing

shut in exhaustion. "No, I will not marry you," she repeated for what felt like the hundredth time in a mere week.

"I will not ask again," Tynan threatened, his fists tightening at his sides.

Irsa fought the urge to shout, *'good!'* at the top of her lungs.

"I'll save you the trouble," Aislin offered softly. "I will not now, nor shall I ever agree to marry you. Please do not ask again."

The prince stormed out, a snarl on his lips, slamming the door behind him. Aislin let out a breath, sinking to the sand, where Irsa moved to embrace her tightly. "Why?" Irsa asked softly.

"He does not love me, he loves the idea of me, and nothing more. He doesn't know me," Aislin whispered back. They stayed there for a long moment, holding one another before returning to work.

GAVRIL RETURNED THE FOLLOWING DAY, with two armed royal guards in tow. He did not knock or wait for Irsa to invite him in. He simply burst through the door, causing it to bang violently against the wall. The bookshelf near the door shook and toppled, spilling books onto the floor.

"Was that entirely necessary?" Irsa asked, annoyed.

"Irsa of Tjena, your trial for the murder of Calypso of Ivar will commence in two days' time. We suggest you ready yourself. If you have not sought council by that time, it will be provided for you." Gavril announced, reading from a scroll that dragged the ground pretentiously. "Tomorrow, we will return to escort you to the cell where you will be kept while you await trial. You have a day to get your affairs in order."

"How very magnanimous of you," Irsa muttered dryly. "I suppose I am to write a will, or something as well in the meantime?"

"A will is recommended. If you are found guilty, you will be taken from the trial and executed," Gavril murmured with smug satisfaction.

"Cheery thought. I should go prepare, shouldn't I?" She quirked a brow, wondering where she might find representation on such short notice, but deciding against giving Gavril the satisfaction of asking.

"Yes. You should." he nodded the smirk on his face, only spreading wider. She turned to go back to her work, thinking they'd get the hint and leave, but Gavril and his thugs seemed intent on staying put and making a nuisance of themselves as much as possible. After a few minutes ignoring them and hoping they'd leave, she turned to them arms crossed over her chest.

"Is that all?"

"Yes. It is." Gavril nodded pleased with himself.

"Good. Now, if you don't mind, I'd appreciate you leaving. I've got plenty to do between now and tomorrow, and you're in the way." She narrowed her eyes on them in annoyance. Her magic stretched forth to open the door for them. "I'm sure you can see your way out, can't you?"

The guards nodded and turned on their fins to leave, but Gavril remained where he was. A slow smile on his features still, amber eyes glittering with malice. "That's right, act smug, but we shall see who's laughing in two days when they strand you on land to suffocate."

"It might still be me, Gavril. But, I guess we'll see, won't we?" Irsa asked, quirking a gray brow in mild amusement.

Her amusement unsettled the burly merman. His lips twitching from their smirk for the first time since entering her shop. "Yes, we will see," he muttered lamely before turning to swim out of her shop.

Once he left, Irsa's shoulders sagged. Her magic reached out to shut the door behind them, and she slumped into a chair. "This is a disaster," she whispered, scrubbing at her face. With a deep inhale, she forced away the sick oncoming dread—now was not the time—rose from her seat and swam over to Aislin's shop. "We need to talk," she announced.

Aislin looked up from the tunic she was mending to frown at her. "What's wrong?"

The short answer, *'a lot.'* But Irsa settled in to relay the story of everything that had happened to her friend. By the time it was all done, Aislin's brows had furrowed in thought. A frown marred that beautiful face of hers, and Irsa waited with bated breath for the tears she was sure would follow.

"Well," Aislin said finally, her frown deepening.

"Well?" Irsa asked when it seemed that Aislin wouldn't say anything else on the subject.

"This is less than ideal," Aislin muttered, biting her full bottom lip.

"Less than ideal," Irsa repeated, her eyes widening. "That seems like an understatement, Aislin. They could execute me for Amphitrite's sake!"

"I caught that, Irsa," Aislin responded calmly, her eyes meeting her friends levelly. "But now is not the time to panic."

"It seems like the perfect time to panic to me," Irsa exclaimed, waving her arms dramatically.

Aislin sighed, reaching out to take her friend's hands and holding them tightly. "Calm down, I'm going to think of a way out of this. I promise."

"How?" Irsa asked weakly.

"Maybe Tynan can help us. He could issue a royal pardon." Although the words were soft, lacking any malice, something within Irsa's chest twisted.

"He won't help me, he has no reason to," Irsa protested.

"He will have a reason," Aislin insisted, a slow but terrifying smile stretching her face. "If I agree to marry him, he'll have no choice but to listen to me. I can get him to pardon you, and you'll be safe."

Irsa's gut wrenched violently. "Aislin, no. There has to be another way," she whispered desperately.

Aislin shook her head, smiling gently. "There is no other way. You need a royal pardon, and he won't do me any favors until I agree to marry him. This is the only way."

"But, what about," Irsa gestured to their shops, to their life that they had built together.

"You can stay here, and I'll visit as often as I can. Or we can convince him to bring you on as the royal sea witch, so we could be together." Aislin's smile was blinding at the very thought. She had figured this all out and would not be dissuaded from the idea.

IN THE MORNING, they sent word to the castle, and Tynan was in the shop within the hour.

"I do not appreciate being summoned," he growled darkly, his bright eyes narrowing on Aislin, who merely smiled serenely in response.

"I apologize, your highness, but I have good news," She swam to him, taking his hands. Irsa watched all of this, her stomach plummeting to the tip of her fin where it may never return from. "I have decided to accept your proposal."

A handsome smile lit the prince's features, and he laughed. "Oh, you have, have you? Well, I'm glad you finally came to your senses. Pack your things, we will leave for the castle at once."

"Yes, of course, darling. But," Aislin started. Her eyes began to glow faintly, so faintly that if Irsa hadn't memorized the exact shade of green they were ages ago, she'd have missed it. "I wonder if, in a gesture of love, you would help my friend, Irsa? The Council is doing everything in its power to have her convicted and executed for a crime she did not commit. A royal pardon would be the perfect engagement present," she cooed softly, compulsion magic flowing from her softly. Irsa's eyes widened, it had been many years since she'd seen Aislin use that power, and it had never once been that strong.

Tynan nodded quickly, freeing one hand to snap at Sebastian. "See that it is done, my merman. I want my new bride to be happy in her new home."

Sebastian, who was floating off to the side, nodded, a frown settling onto his features. His eyes narrowed on Irsa suspiciously. "Yes, Your Highness, I will have the paperwork drawn up immediately. Is there anything else her ladyship desires?" He drawled.

"I wonder if it wouldn't be possible to bring Irsa on, at the castle, as the Royal Sea Witch?" Aislin continued at the prompting, a beautiful smile splitting her features. "She's accomplished and would prove to be a great asset. And since you haven't chosen your sea witch yet... well," Aislin let the words drift off.

"Of course!" Tynan brightened. "Sebastian?"

"Yes, sir."

"Wonderful," Aislin squealed with a happy giggle. She threw herself into the prince's arms and kissed him deeply. Irsa's eyes flicked to the sand, swallowing roughly. It was necessary, but she didn't have to like it. When Aislin pulled back from the kiss, she turned to Irsa. "Since Irsa will pack her own things, perhaps you could have some of your men help her bring everything to the castle, and I can go with you now?"

Tynan nodded quickly, his arm looping around Aislin's waist to pull her in close. "Whatever my lady desires," he murmured, nodding to Sebastian. He turned to lead Aislin outside. Green eyes cast a glance over Aislin's shoulder shooting Irsa a small triumphant smile, and she and the prince disappeared out into the street and into his waiting carriage.

"Don't think I don't see what this is." Sebastian growled darkly to Irsa once they were out of earshot.

Irsa quirked a brow. "I don't know what you're talking about."

"I will be watching you. Both of you," he warned.

Irsa responded with a shrug before following the newly engaged couple into the street so she could head up to their apartment and begin packing up their happy little life.

Chapter Thirteen

*T*hat very evening, Janette reappeared at Irsa's door, a scroll sticking out of her messenger bag. "It's been a while," Irsa breathed, opening the door for the other merwoman.

"It has," Janette agreed, swimming inside. She settled into the offered seat, setting the scroll on the table.

"Shall I make us some tea?" Irsa offered.

"No, thank you." Janette waved her off. "I've come to tell you that your royal pardon was received, and the Council will no longer be taking action against you for Calypso's death." Although the news she brought was technically good, Janette's tone was grave.

"But?" Irsa asked, settling at the table across from the girl she may have once called a friend.

"Its as if every time I visit you, it is to bring bad tidings," Janette muttered to herself, shaking her head. She took a deep breath and nodded. "But you have made some powerful enemies within the ranks of the Council. For many years Gavril had his eye on the position of the royal sea witch, and you've stolen it from under him."

Irsa snorted, rolling her eyes. "I don't think I have anything to worry about from Gavril."

Janette frowned more, shaking her head. "He may not have as much magic at his disposal as you do Irsa, but he's not above dirty tactics. He didn't get into the position he's in without hurting people, and you've infuriated him."

"And what? You think I should snub the opportunity to save a pretentious merman his pride?" Irsa asked incredulously.

"No," Janette laughed bitterly, shaking her head.

"Then what?"

"I'm only asking that you swim lightly. Gavril has friends in the castle who could make things hard for you. And with your... predilection," Janette murmured.

Irsa quirked a brow. "My predilection?"

With a huff, Janette shook her head. "You don't hide it very well that you're in love with Aislin, a fact you know is not legal in Alon, and even less so now that she is the prince's betrothed. So, I'd be careful if I were you."

Irsa nodded, frowning thoughtfully. "I see. Well, thank you for the warning, Janette. I'll keep it in mind."

Janette nodded, rising from her chair. "This is your pardon," she said handing Irsa the scroll. "Good luck, old friend." She spun on her fin and left Irsa to her thoughts.

IRSA HAD NEVER IMAGINED that packing up her small, but happy life into a few crates would be so difficult. She had always believed that when they left their small apartment, another kingdom would be on the horizon and they would be together. But here she was loading everything into boxes, and feeling strangely hollow. Still, their tiny life was boxed up and ready to be shipped to the palace in a few

Tales of a Sea Witch

short days. She followed shortly after, off to start her life anew once more.

Settling into the large office, the prince's men directed her to was strangely easy by comparison. There was so much space that it dwarfed even Calypso's expansive library. Irsa lowered the first crate of books to the sand in the middle of the room, doing a quick spin to take in the office and decide where it was, she wanted to put everything.

"Plenty of room to grow. We must go book shopping," Aislin's voice drew her attention. Her friend was leaning against the doorframe, clad in a sand-length glittering white gown, and a cheeky grin.

"And the prince would sponsor such an expedition," Irsa teased, a smile splitting her lips.

"Well, of course he will! You are the royal sea witch. You need all the books you can get, obviously." Aislin swam to her friend, taking her hands and squeezing them. "I am so glad you're here, with me."

Irsa nodded, returning the squeeze. The weight that had been resting heavily on her chest since Janette had visited lift. Gavril and his vendetta, forgotten in the wake of this playful teasing. In that moment, they were simply Irsa and Aislin again. It was effortless.

***

IRSA REALIZED QUICKLY THAT, without the fear of being found out looming over them at all times, that's how it was now. She and Aislin were finally free to be themselves. In the castle's safety, they could laugh and play for the first time since they had been children.

Irsa hardly saw the prince, and it seemed neither did Aislin. He was always too busy, off attending to some urgent matter or another. That left his bride in the hands of his new sea witch.

After nearly six months in the castle, Aislin was still unwed, and Irsa was still free to spend her days, however, she chose. Occasionally she would work for the king, enough to earn her position as sea witch, but mostly it felt that Tynan had only brought her to the palace to act as a companion to Aislin. Of which Irsa would not complain, for she enjoyed their time together too much. One thing was perfectly clear during that time though, Aislin loved being a princess. She thrived on the splendor that was the palace and the attention of the staff. She was born to be royalty, and Irsa would not stand in her way.

Irsa had nearly forgotten that Aislin was engaged at all when Aislin came rushing into her office in a flutter of bubbles and giggles. "It's set," she announced proudly, before squealing loudly.

"What's set?" Irsa asked, looking up from her desk, her brows raised.

"The date." When Aislin didn't get the response she wanted, she huffed, rolling her eyes at Irsa. "For my wedding. My royal wedding. Oh Irsa, it will be so beautiful!"

It all came crashing back in an instant. That was why they were here in the castle. Aislin was not some princess, free to do what she wished with whoever she wished it. She was betrothed to the future king of Alon, and Irsa was nothing more than the prince's sea witch. "Right, your wedding," Irsa whispered. She'd thought she'd had more time. So much more time. Still, she forced a smile. "When is the happy day?" She asked.

"A month! Only a month! Oh, my, Irsa there is so much to do! And you'll help, of course. You have to help. I want you to make my dress, and be my maid of honor, and I'll need you to swim me down the aisle. Do you think that'll be all right?" Aislin asked, not seeing the heartbreak in her friend's eyes as she was wrapped up in her own excitement.

"Whatever you want Aislin." Irsa laughed softly, letting the infectious excitement seep into her too. It was easier than facing the truth that she may lose her friend forever, too soon.

"Perfect! It will be perfect!" Aislin laughed, swimming to her to hug her tightly. "You are the absolute best friend, and I love you so much." She giggled.

ALTHOUGH PLANNING a wedding for Aislin to another mer left Irsa feeling consistently gutted, she went on with it. This was what Aislin wanted. She was thriving there in the palace. Irsa could not stand between Aislin and whatever future happiness being the queen of Alon would bring her. Still, Irsa wished it were she that Aislin would swim down the aisle towards.

Aislin's bubbly, happy mood continued for much of the month, which was the only thing that kept Irsa going. Then one night about a week before the wedding, as they poured over the seating arrangements, Aislin's mood took a drastic swing for the serious. She looked up from the scroll before her, and asked, "Irsa, do you think I'm making a mistake?"

Black eyes met green, Irsa blinked in confusion. "A mistake?"

"By marrying Tynan. Am I doing the right thing?" Aislin clarified.

There was a foolish, naive, broken part of Irsa that wanted to grab her friend and shake her. To scream in her face that '*yes, dear Poseidon, yes you are making a mistake!*' She swallowed it down. It would do neither of them any good to feed into this sudden melancholy mood. "You love him, Aislin, how could there be any mistake?"

Aislin said no more, she merely ducked her head back to the seating arrangements, and they continued on as if nothing had been said.

THE DAY of the wedding arrived with no further mishap. Aislin was a bundle of nerves and excitement. Everything had to be perfect, and she needed Irsa to make sure it was. So Irsa spent much of the morning swimming from place to place making sure everyone was on time and accounted for before heading to the bridal suite to help Aislin finish getting ready for the wedding.

"You look stunning," Irsa whispered, adjusting the veil. She bent down to press a kiss to the crown of Aislin's head, smiling softly. It was true, Aislin looked heartbreakingly beautiful, and Irsa's breath stuttered at the sight of her. Aislin smiled back at her in the mirror. Suddenly her smile faltered, and her expression soured. Irsa blinked at her in confusion before asking, "What is it?"

"I know I promised to do this," Aislin whispered. "And that originally I agreed to it to protect you." She took Irsa's hand, giving it a squeeze before she pulled it closer to press a kiss to the inside of Irsa's wrist. "But is all of this a mistake?"

Irsa shook her head, inhaled deeply through her nose, and out again to steel herself for what she had to say next. "No, I don't think so. You're happier here than I've ever seen you. You really were meant to be a princess. And Tynan cares for you," Irsa insisted.

"Not the way you do."

"No, his way is different," Irsa agreed. "But different

isn't always bad, and perhaps things will change after the wedding. Perhaps you'll become closer?"

Aislin nodded, closing her eyes. "He is rather handsome," she smiled a little.

"Yes. I suppose he is."

"But you are rather beautiful." she opened her eyes to smile at Irsa in the mirror. "Promise you won't leave me?" Aislin begged.

"I promise," Irsa whispered, unable to say anything but even when it might be an impossible promise to keep. It was something more than a promise, it was a vow.

Aislin giggled, tugging Irsa down into her lap by her wrist and kissing her deeply for the first time in years. There was a not-so-subtle tug on Irsa's heart, but she fought it. Now was not the time.

AFTER THE KISS, the rest of the wedding was a complete blur. Irsa merely went through the motions of swimming Aislin down the aisle and saying her well-practiced toast. It didn't matter. None of it mattered, because although Aislin had married that trussed up lobster for a prince, it was nothing near what she and Aislin now shared. Their connection went soul deep, something the prince would never have or understand.

The wedding went off without a hitch, and Irsa waited for her chance to see Aislin again. She knew it wouldn't be immediately. Aislin would have new duties as wife and princess that she needed to see to. Irsa bided her time, continued working, and waited.

Irsa sat behind her desk some months later, her eyes staring down at the book before her, but not reading the words at all.

A soft knock drew her attention, and there floating in the doorway was Aislin, a little smile on her face. "Irsa," she whispered, cheeks flushing.

"Aislin," Irsa smiled brightly, rising from her chair to swim over her desk. She swam to Aislin, taking her hands and pulling her into a tight hug.

"Irsa!" Aislin laughed, hugging her back. "Where have you been keeping yourself?" She teased lightly.

Irsa shook her head, laughing. "No, my dear princess, where have *you* been keeping *yourself*?" She pulled back to get a better look at Aislin.

A little frown tugged at Aislin's lips at the words, and she sighed. "I'm sorry. I wanted to. But Tynan has kept me so busy, and I just—" she broke off, inhaling deeply once more. "I didn't know how to face you."

"Face me?" Irsa asked, her stomach twisting at the uncertainty in Aislin's voice. "Why would it be hard to face me?"

Aislin tugged her by her hands over to the long couch along the wall and sat facing her on it. She reached out to brush Irsa's cheek gently, her smile still full of uncertainty. "I wasn't sure that you'd want anything to do with me after I kissed you and ran off to marry the prince."

"Aislin," Irsa sighed, tugging her in closer. "I understand. I understand that you felt you had to. There was little choice there for either of us. I understand." She whispered the words soothingly.

Aislin's shoulders relaxed, and she sighed, relieved. "While we're on the topic of that kiss—" Aislin drifted off, pulling a silver ring from her pocket. "I wanted to-to ask you something," she stumbled a little, her cheeks flushing brightly.

"Calm down Aislin, it's me, just ask." Irsa encouraged softly, giving her a smile.

With a deep fortifying breath, Aislin continued. "You promised me you'd never leave me, right?"

Irsa nodded. "Yes, I remember."

"I wonder if you'd-you'd swear?" Aislin whispered uncertainly. "Swear to never leave me. Swear to be by my side until Amphitrite calls us home?" She fiddled with the ring nervously. "I've known for quite some time now. You're my-you're my soul mate and I don't want to ever be without you again."

"I swear," Irsa whispered, her eyes meeting Aislin's earnestly. "I won't leave you. I'll remain by your side until Amphitrite calls us home," she repeated the words back to Aislin, smiling softly.

A delighted giggle left Aislin as she slipped the ring onto Irsa's little finger. Then leaned forward to hug Irsa tightly. "Oh, Irsa, I love you so much. I can't even explain it."

Irsa chuckled, gently pushing Aislin back so their eyes could meet again, before she leaned in and pressed her lips to Aislin's, pouring everything she felt in that moment, and always had into it. She allowed Aislin to feel the heartache, and love, and desperation she felt to the tip of her fin. She savored the way their bond hummed between them at the connection.

When she pulled back, they were both panting and smiling like mad. "But I don't have anything for you," Irsa blurted, and the pair dissolved into ridiculous giggles.

"Good thing I brought an extra," Aislin winked at her, pulling another little ring from her pocket and holding it out to her. Irsa slipped it onto the little freckled finger and pulled Aislin into her again. They stayed that way, enjoying the closeness.

Chapter Fourteen

*I*t was surprisingly easy to have an affair with the newlywed princess of Alon. Her husband, Prince Tynan, spent much of his time busy in meetings or tending to matters of state, and seemed to have little time for a wife. The whole of the castle had accepted that the pair were the best of friends. No one even batted an eyelash when they saw them swimming through the halls holding hands, or when Aislin spent hours upon hours holed up in Irsa's office.

The palace was the perfect place for a budding romance. The couple swam through the gardens, went seahorse riding around the grounds, enjoyed jellyfish-lit dinners together, and found many hidey-holes to tuck themselves away from prying eyes.

It was so effortless that Janette's warnings to watch her back were far from Irsa's mind. She'd entirely forgotten about them until one day when she was escorting a particularly rumpled Aislin from her office, she found Sebastian waiting right outside the door. Irsa and Aislin stopped, blinking at the merman in confusion.

"Your Majesty," he murmured, bowing deeply at the waist to Aislin, who continued to blink at him. "I trust you are well?"

"I-uh-yes, quite well," Aislin answered, her cheeks flushing brightly.

He rose from the bow, a little smile tugging at the corner of his lips as if he'd caught her doing something she oughtn't. "Then why, may I ask, are you with the sea witch?"

"I'm visiting with my friend," Aislin said, finally recovered from her initial shock. She straightened her spine, meeting Sebastian's eye dead on, her chin lifting.

"Yes, you seem to visit with your friend frequently," Sebastian murmured knowingly. Irsa's scales bristled at the insinuation, even if what he was implying was precisely right.

"And what business is that of yours?" Irsa asked, her hands clenching into fists at her sides, magic sparking from them dangerously.

Sebastian quirked one brow, his expression turning smug. "Oh, I thought as the prince's most trusted friend and advisor, it might behoove me to keep track of his wife and her goings-on in the castle. Since he's so busy as of late." He shrugged.

"So, spying," Irsa blurted. "You're spying on her."

"Is it spying if there is nothing to see?" He asked, tilting his head to one side as if inspecting Irsa.

"You ought to show your future queen more respect, you insolent li—" Irsa shouted, only stopping when Aislin held up a hand to silence her.

"Of course, it's not. Thank you for checking on me, Sebastian, but I am quite all right, as you can see. And now that I have finished visiting my friend, I'm going to head to my meeting. Excuse me." Aislin ducked her head out of respect and swam away, leaving Irsa and Sebastian floating together fin to fin.

Once she was out of earshot, Sebastian returned his attention to Irsa. "You ought to be more careful little witch. I told you I'd be watching you."

"Yes, a thinly veiled threat, but as Aislin said, we were merely visiting." Irsa's calm had returned, and she met Sebastian with her own breed of smug satisfaction. "So, there really is nothing to watch me for."

"The prince may accept this little arrangement the three of you have but don't think for a second that the people of Alon would. If this were to become common knowledge," Sebastian let his words trail off, a little smirk tugging at his lips. "Well, I think we all know what he'd do, don't we?"

Irsa's belly did a sick twist, but she swallowed it down as best as she was able. "And what—pray tell—would they find out? As we said, we're friends."

"Of course. Of course. Very good friends," Sebastian nodded, turning on his fin. "Word of advice, don't let your little tryst make you forget who her husband is," he called over his shoulder as he swam down the hall. "Good night Irsa."

Irsa's tail flicked as she headed back to her office. She leaned against the door, taking deep gulps of water to steady herself. Sebastian might be right, they needed to be more careful. But some part of her wondered if he was only saying that to scare them. To drive a wedge between them and weasel his way in somehow. Either way, she'd make a note to keep their meetings a secret. Even if that meant that they weren't able to do some things they had been enjoying doing together. Like seahorse riding or strolling through the halls holding hands.

Tales of a Sea Witch

SINCE HER RUN-IN WITH SEBASTIAN, Irsa's stomach had been in knots. She took to spinning the little silver ring around her pinky to soothe herself, and it helped mostly. But still she insisted to Aislin that they must keep their meetings secluded to her office. At least then they could make up some lie about a stomachache, or a headache which had led her to seek a tincture from the palace witch.

Seclusion with Aislin didn't chafe as much as Irsa thought it might. The hours they wiled away, curled up on the plush sofa in her office made it feel as if the ocean outside those walls had ceased to exist. It was she and Aislin, no one else.

One evening as Aislin sat with her back to Irsa's chest, her fingers toying with the little silver ring on Irsa's gray-brown finger Aislin asked, "Do you think he'll be king one day?"

Irsa frowned a little, they never spoke of Tynan and his place as the rightful heir, but she supposed it would have to come up at some point. "Yes, I think he will. King Hemnes would have to die first though, I don't see him stepping down." They were both power-mad, in Irsa's mind, neither seemed capable of stepping down to let a younger generation rise.

"Perhaps King Hemnes will outlive him, and I'll be a princess forever." Aislin laughed suddenly, a delirious note to the words.

Irsa sighed, holding Aislin tighter. "You don't want to be queen?"

Aislin took a long time to answer, then shook her head. "No, a queen has to give her king an heir. A princess can run around with the palace sea witch behind closed doors," she whispered thoughtfully.

"You don't have to be either if you don't want," Irsa insisted earnestly.

"Either what?" Aislin asked as if she were only half-listening.

"You don't have to be a princess or a queen if you don't want. We can run away together—like we always planned—and you could be a seamstress again. You'd have to give up all the frills, though," Irsa teased, gently bumping her nose to the back of Aislin's bare neck. She placed a long, lingering kiss just there.

"He'd never let me," Aislin whispered, sadly. "But the longer we prolong me being queen, the longer I can prolong having an heir."

Irsa nodded in understanding, doing her best to provide comfort to Aislin by holding her and pressing her face to the back of Aislin's neck. "We'll figure it out one day, I promise. We have plenty of time," Irsa murmured against her skin, and Aislin seemed to relax at her words.

"Together?" Aislin asked.

"Always, together," Irsa promised.

For months, nothing changed. It seemed as if Irsa and Aislin had all the time in the world to think up a new plan of escape. Irsa hoarded away every clamshell she made, taking on odd jobs outside of the castle to bring in extra money, in case. Aislin kept a small cache of gifts from the prince to barter for their safe passage if it came to that. They had to work slowly to avoid suspicion. Still, Irsa was reasonably sure that they'd have enough to escape before King Hemnes died. Prince Tynan played his part perfectly; he was much too busy maneuvering himself politically to notice what his wife and sea witch were doing. This left Aislin and Irsa plenty of time to plot and enjoy one another's company.

"I want to go on a date," Aislin announced one day when she swam into Irsa's office. Her smile bright, and her eyes twinkling with amusement.

Irsa looked up from the papers on her desk she'd been pouring over—most of which were requests for potions and tinctures by the other residents of the castle. She wrinkled her nose a little as the words sank in. "A date?"

"A date," Aislin confirmed with a firm nod. "Like humans do in my books." She swam to Irsa's desk, setting a novel on it with a soft thunk. "Where they go to dinner and talk, and hold hands, and such."

Water filled her lungs on a deep inhale before Irsa shook her head. "I don't think that's a good idea, Aislin. We're supposed to be lying low, remember? We don't want Sebastian to get more suspicious and tell everyone about us." It was a reasonable concern, but Irsa knew what happened when Aislin had made up her mind.

"Oh, come on, Irsa. No one will see us. We'll go far out to the edge of the city where no one will recognize us," Aislin insisted. "It'll be safe, I promise," she swore. Irsa eyed her skeptically, but she relented before the next plea left Aislin's lips. "Please," Aislin begged with a pleading smile, her eyes going wide and guppy like.

"All right," Irsa sighed heavily. "What kind of date do you want?"

"Dinner?" Aislin grinned brightly.

"Dinner," Irsa nodded. "I'll need some time to plan it. Give me a few days?"

"Of course!" Aislin giggled, spinning on her fin to head back out of the office with a broad smile on her lips.

With a fond shake of her head, Irsa looked back down to the requests on her desk. Many of them she approved, but there was one from Prince Tynan for a particular seagrass that was strange. Instead of accepting it, she set up a meeting with the prince to discuss it further.

THE REQUEST from the prince slipped from Irsa's mind in favor of planning her date with Aislin, and a few days later, everything was set. She had convinced the guards that would be on duty to leave the entrance into the kitchens unattended, chosen a restaurant far out of the way. She found them both cloaks that would make them as inconspicuous as possible.

All that was left was to choose the perfect outfit, something that would impress Aislin, and hopefully leave her as breathless as Irsa frequently found herself. After much hemming and hawing, Irsa decided on a short purple gown. She straightened it in the mirror, smiled at herself, brushing a short lock of silvery gray hair back from her face. She was no prince, but she felt beautiful.

She headed down to the kitchens to wait for Aislin to meet her. Thank Amphitrite, Aislin did not keep her waiting at all. When Irsa arrived, Aislin was bobbing nervously at the door to the kitchens. Her long brown cloak pulled over her red hair to hide it. Pale, freckled fingers twisted in the braid of hair pulled over her shoulder.

Swimming quietly towards her, Irsa couldn't help but smile. "Did you think I'd stand you up?" She asked softly, her hands reaching out to still Aislin's.

Aislin lifted her head to meet Irsa's eyes. The smile splitting her features made Irsa's heart stutter, and she smiled back. "Only a little," Aislin laughed.

"Silly girl," Irsa chided teasingly, her thumbs rubbing soothing circles on Aislin's hands. "Come on, before the guards come back," she whispered conspiratorially.

She nodded, Aislin allowed Irsa to pull her down the grimy, dank servant's entrance of the castle out into the city that surrounded it. Once they ducked down another alley, and the castle was out of sight, Irsa found herself able to breathe a little easier. Out in the city, they were Irsa and Aislin again. No one cared who they were or what they did so long as they weren't bothering anyone. They were free.

"This way," Irsa whispered quickly, tugging Aislin down another dimly lit side street. Aislin giggled as they wound their way through back alleys and poorly lit streets until they reached the edge of the city where the castle was completely obscured from view. Although Irsa saw it was only an illusion, it seemed that they had outstretched the prince's reach at last. There, he could not touch them. There, it were as if that the shining carriage and glittery castle were all parts of a nightmare cooked up by too many sweets before bed.

"Where are we going?" Aislin asked with an excited giggle.

"You'll see," Irsa murmured evasively, tugging her out of the way of a passing carriage. When they finally arrived, Irsa pulled them to a stop, looking up at the restaurant. Tucked into the very edge of the city, the small building was unassuming. It wasn't anything fancy, but the food was good, and that's all that mattered to Irsa.

"Is this the big surprise?" Aislin asked, looking up at the building, her hood falling back away from her face. Irsa looked over at Aislin, and her heart stuttered. Aislin had lined her eyes in squid ink and sprinkled jellyfish glitter along her cheekbones. Her long red hair was twisted into a braid littered with glittering jewels. She was stunning.

"No, this is just a stop," Irsa answered, finding it harder to breathe than usual.

"What is the big surprise?" Aislin looked over at her, brows raised.

"You'll have to wait and see," Irsa smirked, then she took Aislin's hand and led her inside. Once inside, Irsa dropped her hand, leaving Aislin to float by the door and swam to the hostess. "I'm here to pick up an order under the name Irsa," she informed her in a soft murmur.

The girl nodded quickly, spinning to disappear into the kitchen for a long moment. When she returned, she was struggling with a large basket. "I think this is everything," she grunted, holding it out to Irsa.

"I'm sure it is," Irsa offered her a broad smile. She reached out with one glittering, magical tentacle to take the basket from her and turned to Aislin. "Come along dear, we've still got to rent a seahorse."

"A seahorse?" Aislin asked, following her out into the street again. "Irsa, where are we going?"

"You'll see, trust me," Irsa muttered. They headed to a little stable a block away, and Irsa paid for them to rent a seahorse and a small cart. Once they and their basket were loaded, Irsa steered the seahorse to the city limits and beyond. Aislin's barrage of questions eventually died down as they rode out into the open sea, and they rode on in silence.

An hour into their journey, they finally reached their destination, the Jellyfish Forest. Without a word, Irsa reached out for the basket with a tentacle of magic and helped Aislin from the cart. Aislin raised her brows but didn't ask as Irsa led her into the forest, only Irsa's glittering purple magic lighting their way. She settled the basket to the sand, Irsa pulled a blanket from it to spread out, and tugged Aislin down to sit next to her.

"Irsa, what's going on?" Aislin asked again.

"Shh," Irsa hushed, drawing her magic back into herself

Tales of a Sea Witch

and plunging them into total darkness. Aislin yelped, throwing her arms around Irsa. "Shh," Irsa repeated, stroking Aislin's hair back softly. "Give it a moment," she promised.

They sat in silence, waiting for what seemed like forever. First one tiny jellyfish came out from hiding, its body glowing in the darkness above them. Then another. Then another. And suddenly, the water above them was lit with a million tiny jellyfish, each glowing and moving with the current.

"In that book you showed me, they had a picnic under the stars," Irsa explained. "This isn't quite stars, but—" she shrugged.

"It's perfect," Aislin's words left her in a breathy whisper. She leaned in to kiss Irsa, holding her tightly, and pushing every other thought from Irsa's mind. When Aislin finally pulled back, it was to giggle happily. "This is better than I hoped."

Nodding dumbly with flushed cheeks, Irsa began to unpack the basket so they could enjoy their dinner. For hours the ocean narrowed to a pinprick; there was nothing beyond that blanket. They ate and laughed, and Irsa felt herself falling more and more under Aislin's spell than ever before.

Chapter Fifteen

The following day, Irsa returned to her office to find the overstuffed tuna of a prince was sitting at her desk, his hands clasped before him. A yelp nearly left her at his sudden appearance, but she hid it well beneath a cough. "Irsa, how delightful to see you again," he crooned, gesturing to a seat in front of her desk. "Please, sit, I'd love to have a chat with you."

Eyes narrowed on him suspiciously, Irsa settled into a chair, her fingers clenched together in her lap. "Your Highness, this is unexpected," she offered, pulling on a forced, polite smile. "What do I owe the pleasure?"

"You requested a meeting with me after rejecting my petition for a particular seagrass. So, I'm here to follow up on the matter," Tynan's tone remained polite as well, but there was a sharpness to his smile that made Irsa's hair stand on end. "May I ask why you rejected it?"

Irsa nodded, ignoring the unsettling twist of her stomach. "Of course, Your Highness. As you may not be aware, that seagrass is toxic to merfolk and thus heavily regulated. I would be remiss to hand it over to anyone—

even the crown prince—without an in-person discussion first."

"Ah, yes, we must be cautious with such things." The prince smiled graciously. "I completely understand. But now that we've talked, perhaps you'll reconsider my request?"

"Yes, after you tell me what you plan to use it for," Irsa continued.

"Nothing at all you need trifle yourself with, Irsa," Tynan assured, his voice smooth.

"I'm afraid I really must insist on knowing the use, Your Highness." Her voice was firm. This was not a battle she'd win; if the prince wanted something, he would get it. But she at least had to try. She needed to learn what he was planning in case she needed to protect Aislin from it.

Tynan's eyes narrowed on her, barely restrained fury simmering in their depths. He was not used to being disobeyed, and this did not sit well with him. "You are happy in your position here as Sea Witch, are you not?" He asked.

"Yes, sir, I am."

"And you are pleased with your proximity to my wife?" He quirked a turquoise brow, a knowing smile settling onto his features. "You enjoy spending time with her, do you not?"

She shifted uncomfortably in her chair. Tynan hadn't said as much, but the threat was there. Either Irsa did as he asked, or he would see that she was expelled from the castle and barred from seeing Aislin ever again. He didn't need words to express that; it was all there in his eyes. "Yes, sir," she answered once more.

"I don't think it at all pertinent for you to know the details of my plans, as I am the prince and heir of Alon. Do you?"

"No, sir," she whispered, her shoulders sagging in submission.

He nodded, pleased. "I'm glad we have come to an understanding. Please retrieve the ingredient I requested."

Irsa rose from her chair to do just that, without another word. Her hands shook when she held the vial over to the prince, and he left with a self-satisfied smile on his features.

THEY FOUND the king dead in the gardens not long after. After a short-lived investigation, the Council determined that King Hemnes had suffered an attack of the heart—no further research was needed. They set Tynan's coronation date the very next day before they even buried the king. Irsa's ocean began to slip through her fingers like sand.

The funeral was held a few short days later, and they ushered in a new era with the prince and his wife the very next day. Aislin's duties as queen were at least double what they had been as princess, and Irsa found they had less and less time to spend together. Tynan consistently dragged her along to political meetings and other affairs of state so she could sit by his side—the little pearl he'd plucked from the sand.

"So much for being a princess forever," Aislin sighed, slumping down onto the couch in Irsa's office a month later. She curled into Irsa's arms, pressing her face to the sea witch's shoulder. "Those meetings are so boring. Why does he even need me there?" She complained.

"I know Aislin," Irsa soothed, her fingers brushing Aislin's hair back from her face. "But you're queen now, and that's queens do."

"I realize that," Aislin huffed sullenly. She cuddled

deeper into Irsa's embrace, willing away the ocean outside of her arms.

"I know, Aislin," Irsa repeated. "But at least I'm still here?"

"Thank Amphitrite for that," Aislin whispered, and complained no more. They spent the rest of their time together in silence, enjoying the few fleeting moments they'd been given to be together.

TYNAN WAS SO WRAPPED up in asserting himself as king he hadn't time for his queen outside of her use as arm candy. His inability to balance both was the only small blessing Amphitrite had allowed them, and Irsa thanked the goddess for it every day. Life was not perfect, but it was as close to it as they could ask.

Still, things never remained the same for long, and one day Aislin barged into Irsa's office and said words that stopped her heart. "He is demanding we consummate our marriage and produce an heir."

Irsa stilled, looking up from her work to frown at Aislin. They had known this day would come. Irsa had hoped they'd have more time. "You two have already consummated your marriage, haven't you?" Irsa asked in confusion.

"No, we have not," Aislin answered a look of disgust, overtaking her face. "I never wanted to," she whispered, slumping down onto Irsa's couch as she often did when distressed. "I'm not—you know—attracted to him in that way."

"You're not?" Irsa couldn't help the question; she'd always wondered. Although she understood that she and Aislin shared something special, she'd been under no delusion that Aislin didn't share that with the prince as well. It had always seemed that Aislin was fluid in her intimacy.

"He's handsome," Aislin offered with a shrug. "But I need more than handsome."

Irsa nodded in understanding. "Then, we'll go."

"Go?" Aislin sat up, her eyes widening. "Go where?"

"Anywhere. We'll leave Alon. We'll run out into the open sea—if we have to—so long as it's not here." It had away been at the back of their minds—running away—something they were preparing for but hoped they might never have to do. But now, it seemed, Tynan had forced their hand.

"No," Aislin sighed, scrubbing at her face.

"No?"

"No, he'll chase us, and when he catches us, he'll have you executed for treason. I can't ask you to take that risk," Aislin whispered.

"You're not asking; I'm offering," Irsa argued.

"The answer is still no." Aislin lifted her chin in determination, meeting Irsa's eyes.

"What are we going to do, Aislin? You can't just—" Irsa gestured wildly, her hands beginning to shimmer with magic as she grew more distressed. Aislin moved to her, taking her hands to calm her.

"I can, and I will. I'll give him an heir, and he'll have no further use for me. You and I can go away somewhere." Aislin promised. "Wherever we want. We can build a seahorse farm or move to another kingdom. Adopt every abandoned merbabe under the sea. Whatever we want," Aislin whispered, her eyes bright with the words.

Irsa nodded. She didn't like this idea, but Aislin had set her mind to it. "Soon?"

"A year at most," Aislin swore. "Then I'm all yours." Her hands lifted to cup Irsa's cheeks softly, and she kissed her with everything she had. Irsa's fin curled. They would make this work, somehow.

THE FOLLOWING evening when Irsa's office door opened again, she looked up expecting to find a flustered Aislin, but found the self-important blue tang of a prince. "Your Highness," Irsa rose from her seat to bow respectfully. "Is there something I can do for you this fine evening?"

Tynan swam silently over to the chairs on the other side of her desk and settled into one. Once there, he smiled at her and said, "I hope so, Irsa, I hope so."

She sat up straighter. "What is it, Your Highness?"

"I'm sure Aislin has told you we plan to try for an heir soon," he said conversationally, his hands folding in his lap as his teal tail swished pensively.

"She has, yes," Irsa agreed.

He nodded. "Then it should not surprise you that I'd like her to bear me a son as soon as possible. I'm sure both of you would agree that to expedite the process would be in everyone's best interest?"

"But I'm really not seeing what all this has to do with me," Irsa responded, her brows furrowing. "What you two do in the privacy of your quarters is between —"

"I want a spell or potion to ensure that she bears me a son, immediately," Tynan cut her off.

"I-I-I'm sorry?" Irsa asked, her stomach twisting into knots. "You want what?"

"I've heard nothing but good things about how you helped the women that lived around you when they needed you most. I only ask that you do the same for Aislin now." His tone was fair, reasonable even. And perhaps he thought his request was reasonable, but she knew better.

"I can't do that." Irsa frowned, her hands tightening into fists on top of her desk.

"Why not? You helped all of those women? Why can't you help your friend now?" He asked, ire rising in his tone.

"I helped them get pregnant. I ensured they were safe and healthy throughout their entire pregnancy and their labor. I even looked after the children when they were first born. But I cannot determine the gender of a child. That is something entirely up to Amphitrite herself. And any attempts to do so would endanger the mother and child." Irsa's words were soft but serious. This was not something she would budge on, for she knew the dangers well enough.

"Have you ever tried it?" He asked.

"No, of course not. But every sea witch knows it is not to be done. There are dire consequences for fooling with nature," Irsa frowned more deeply.

"So, it's not impossible," he continued.

"Your Highness, I need not try something to understand that it is dangerous. We do not go to the surface for fear of what the humans would do to us, because we recognize them to be dangerous. Not every merperson needs to see that for themselves," she argued.

"You will do this," he insisted.

"I will not."

"You will do this, or I will expose that you helped me to assassinate my father." His voice had turned cold and demanding, his eyes narrowing to slits.

Irsa's mouth opened and closed at the threat, unable to think of a retort.

This seemed to satisfy him, so he nodded. "Aislin will see you every week for regular treatments to ensure she bears me a son, and that she and my child are safe. I'm certain that since you love her as I do, you will do everything in your power to protect her." Tynan smiled sharply, rising from his chair. "Good night, Irsa."

Irsa didn't breathe until the door shut behind him. Panic overwhelmed her. She needed to get Aislin as far from Alon as she was able — now.

Chapter Sixteen

Irsa found Aislin in the gardens the next day. She rushed to her, taking her hands and squeezing them. "We have to go — now," she whispered urgently.

Aislin blinked at her, laughing. "Go? Go where?"

"We have to leave the castle; we have to leave Alon. We have to get as far from Tynan as we can — immediately," Irsa rushed, her eyes wide with panic. "It's not safe for us here any longer."

Aislin frowned, looking around to see if anyone was watching, before she tugged Irsa into an alcove in the garden. "What's wrong?"

A sob wracked Irsa's chest as she told Aislin everything from her conversation with the prince. She scrubbed at her eyes for a moment, then looked at Aislin, hoping her friend would agree that they needed to go. They should get out while they still could.

But Aislin merely sighed. "We can't leave," she whispered, brokenly. "We have to stay."

"But—"

Aislin silenced Irsa with her lips before pulling back to offer her a serene smile. "You're the most powerful sea witch in all of Alon. You have brought many children into the ocean. And you are my heart and soul; I trust you, Irsa. You will take care of me," she whispered with blind faith. "One," she insisted. "That's all we need—one son. We can do that."

"Aislin—I don't think—" Irsa whispered, her shoulders shaking.

"I'm strong enough," Aislin promised.

IRSA WENT BACK to her office and poured over her library of books for two days straight until she found a solution that she thought would be reasonably safe for Aislin. There were no guarantees that it would work, but Aislin would survive the attempt. She spent the next week working on the potion, barely sleeping.

When the time finally came to administer it for the first time, Irsa settled heavily onto the couch with Aislin. "I'm not sure if it'll work," she whispered.

"All we can do is try," Aislin encouraged with a nod.

"Yes, all we can do is try," Irsa agreed. "It will hurt and leave you exhausted, but I'll be here with you. And I'm going to use every bit of our bond to share it with you if I can. You won't have to endure it entirely." She took Aislin's hand, murmuring softly, the shimmering purple magic reaching out from her to Aislin. It twisted and wove its way up Aislin's arm to her chest, settling there with a pleasant hum of power. "It's the only way I know to keep you safe," Irsa whispered.

"Does it taste disgusting?" Aislin asked, trying to lighten the mood.

The joke tugged a tired smile up Irsa's cheeks. "Probably. But you have to drink all of it, anyway."

Aislin took the vial and downed it in one swift gulp, a shudder running through her at the taste. "Definitely disgusting," she grumbled, blanching.

"How do you feel?" Irsa asked worriedly.

"I'm fine." Aislin smiled. "It will be all right, Irsa, this is going to work," she promised.

"Dear Amphitrite, I pray that it does," Irsa whispered.

THE POTION'S effects were not immediately evident, but once Aislin was pregnant, Irsa saw the true danger in it. Aislin slept frequently, and when she wasn't sleeping, she swam around the castle listlessly. Aislin's usually glowing countenance had dimmed to something barely visible. Irsa felt the weight of it too, her own movements slower than normal as her magic poured into Aislin to keep her alive.

Irsa's heart twisted every time she had to give Aislin another dose.

"Just one more month," Aislin promised weakly, her hand tightening around Irsa's. "I'll be done very soon, and then you and I can go."

Irsa nodded, her eyes prickling with tears. "One more month," she repeated.

Aislin took the next draught in a gulp, her head lowered to rest on Irsa's shoulder, snuggling into her warmth. "It'll be over soon," she murmured.

Irsa's arms tightened around her protectively, her magic reaching out to give Aislin everything she was able. It wasn't much, and it would never be enough to make Aislin herself again. All Irsa could do was pray to Amphitrite that it would be enough to keep Aislin alive for another month.

Tynan didn't bother with Aislin or Irsa for the entire pregnancy, and Sebastian stayed away. Which left them to their own devices, so Irsa gave Aislin the attention she needed. Of which, Irsa was grateful. But she realized that they couldn't do this again. Even if Aislin did not bare the prince a son, there wasn't a chance that they could try this again. "Amphitrite willing, that will be enough," she whispered.

"Hm?" Aislin asked, blinking heavily up at her.

"Nothing, my dear. Go back to sleep," Irsa soothed, brushing her hair back from her face. She leaned in to press her lips to Aislin's forehead, frowning when it was a little warmer than usual.

THROUGH A COMBINATION of Irsa's magic and blessings from Amphitrite, Aislin survived to give birth to the child. When all was done, Aislin lay in the bed, panting raggedly while her child screamed loud enough to wake the entire kingdom of Alon. It wriggled in Irsa's arms, full of energy and life that it had sapped from Aislin. Irsa rocked the child, getting it to sleep eventually, and settling beside Aislin on the bed. Taking Aislin's hand, she reached out with her magic to replenish some of Aislin's.

"Rest, my dear," Irsa whispered. "For tomorrow, we leave." She wrinkled her nose at the little girl in her arms, frowning more. She didn't care what the prince said, in the morning they would be gone. He had his child; he wouldn't force Aislin to do this again.

Aislin woke after a while, smiling up at Irsa. "How is he?" She asked.

"She — is healthy," Irsa corrected, the word turning to

bile in her mouth. She held the baby out to Aislin, letting it rest in her arms.

"She's beautiful," Aislin whispered breathlessly. "But—"

Irsa nodded. "A daughter, not a son."

Aislin whimpered softly, holding the baby closer. "I can't do it again, Irsa," she whispered brokenly.

Inhaling deeply, Irsa nodded. "You won't have to do it again. You and I are leaving. Your daughter will have to suffice for Tynan. He can marry her off to the youngest son of Hejne or something. I don't care. He's not making you do that again." Irsa had made up her mind.

"He'll find us," Aislin insisted, not for the first time.

"Let him try. Let him chase us halfway across the ocean. I'll sell my services to a rival kingdom if I have to, but I'm not subjecting you to that again," Irsa said firmly. She leaned in to press a kiss to Aislin's forehead. "We leave in the morning, pack light."

"Wait Irsa," Aislin caught her hand to stop her from swimming away. "What should I name her?"

Irsa looked down at the babe, now asleep. She was peaceful and beautiful, Irsa found no wonder in those round cheeks, for this child may have been the death of Aislin. "Why don't you name her after one of the seven seas? Fars seems a good enough name."

The baby opened its eyes to blink up at Irsa; then, it cooed softly. "I think she likes it," Aislin murmured, smiling.

"Yes, I suppose she does. May you have a happy life Princess Fars," Irsa whispered, pressing a kiss to the baby's forehead and blessing it with some of her magic. "Now Aislin, I really must get everything ready." Aislin nodded quickly, and Irsa swam from the room. "I'll meet you in my office right before dawn."

Tales of a Sea Witch

IT TOOK Irsa hours to find someone who would sell her a carriage and two seahorses outright, and pack everything they would need for the journey, but she would not rest until they were ready to leave. The two guards whom she had easily bribed for their date were as easy to bribe again. Still, she left nothing to chance; she brewed a sleeping draught to slip into their evening meals. When everything was ready, she returned to her office, where she hoped Aislin would be waiting.

The office was dark, and when she lit the jellyfish lamp on the desk, she found Tynan sitting behind it. Irsa jumped, before leveling a glare at the king. "I'm sure like 'waiting in the dark for people,' was on the list of things royal tutors teach not to do," she muttered sarcastically—all pretense of civility or respect gone. His actions had nearly killed Aislin. Irsa had no respect left for him.

Tynan snorted in amusement at her snipe. "And I think 'stealing the king's wife away to live in a foreign land' was likely on the list of things your tutors advised against." A slow smirk spread his lips as the realization that someone had talked, or heard, dawned on Irsa.

"You can't keep her here, she's her own mer," Irsa argued.

"That's where you're wrong, Irsa. She is my wife, and my queen, I can do whatever I want with her. For years now, you have been useful to me. Your presence made Aislin happy, and all I've ever wanted was her happiness. But it would seem your usefulness has ended. Thus, your appointment in this castle will as well." His words were steady, and even, not laced with even a hint of anger.

"I'm not leaving here without her." Irsa's hands tightened into fists at her sides. She called forth her magic, ready to do whatever she needed to save Aislin.

Tynan quirked one turquoise brow, an impassive smile still on his features. He was infuriatingly calm. "Oh, Irsa, I think you will. If you do not, I will expose both of you for what you are. You will not be welcome anywhere in Alon, and I'll ensure that none of my allies will welcome you either. Should you be caught—and I will catch you—you'll be executed on the spot. A life on the run, is that what you want for Aislin? Never settling, always overshadowed by fear?"

"I could get us out of your reach," Irsa protested. "I have the power to do that."

"Maybe, you would have been able to, if you hadn't poured your energy into Aislin to help her through the pregnancy, you two could have escaped without leaving a trail. But now—" He shook his head tsking softly.

"So what? I'm supposed to leave her to you?" Irsa asked, incredulous.

"Well, I *am* her husband." Tynan shrugged. "But I'll make you a deal, you leave quietly—sever all ties—and when she bears me a son, you can be reunited without ever having to worry that I'll darken your doorstep again."

Irsa growled, tentacles of magic twisting around her.

He held up a hand to silence any further arguments. "Think what Aislin would want," Tynan said diplomatically. "She would want you to be safe."

He was right. Aislin would want Irsa to be safe. She would encourage that they figure out another way. "Very well, but I will return for her."

Tynan nodded, smiling softly. "I'd have it no other way. Now, I'll leave you to your packing. Goodbye, Irsa." He turned to leave, and Irsa did just that. She packed everything she needed, and she left for a small hostel on the outskirts of the city.

There, she reasoned, she was close enough to Aislin to watch over her, but far enough that Tynan would never suspect.

Chapter Seventeen

It took Irsa months to reach Aislin without Tynan noticing their correspondence, but once she had, she vowed never to stop again. What followed was an affair of letters.

The reply arrived a week after Irsa had sent hers.

Irsa,

I am so glad you are safe and healthy. I was worried for you when Tynan said that you had left in the middle of the night, and all that was left was a note. He has not been unkind to me, despite his knowledge of our plan to run away.

And I have glorious news; I'm pregnant again! I pray daily to Amphitrite that she will bless me with a son so you and I can be together again. In the meantime, I hope that you will be safe.

I miss you so.
Yours,
Aislin

Every word was a knife in Irsa's heart, but still, she

wrote back. This latest pregnancy seemed to go more smoothly as Tynan was not using any magic to ensure Aislin bore him a son. And some months later, Aislin gave birth to another baby girl whom she named Larwi.

Irsa,

Amphitrite has blessed me with a second child more beautiful than the first. I've named her Lawri, and I hope you get to meet her one day, you'd love her.

I am much better after this second pregnancy, and it gives me hope that the third will give us a son so you and I can be together once more.

I am happy that you have settled into a new position and are helping people again.

As always, stay safe, my love.

Yours,

Aislin

The months and years stretched between them, bringing Aislin and Tynan four more healthy baby girls. Gavril was named the new Royal Sea Witch, and Irsa watched from the shadows as he paraded about like the king himself.

Irsa,

I am pregnant again. Gavril promises Tynan that his new treatment will ensure I have a son. I hope that he's right, I long to be with you so badly. It's been so long since I saw you. I'm forgetting your face.

I pray to Amphitrite that I'll be with you soon, and I hope that you pray for this child and me.

Yours,

Aislin

The months dragged on, and Aislin's letters became less and less frequent.

Irsa,

I'm sorry it's been so long since last I wrote. I find myself exhausted with the growth of this child. Please forgive me.

Yours,
Aislin

The child was a boy, but he was also stillborn, leaving Aislin devastated. Still, Tynan persuaded her to try again.

Irsa,

He promises this is the last, and if we do not have a son this time, he'll let me go and find a new bride. Gavril has increased my dosage of the tincture to ensure another boy. I am on bed rest until I give birth to make sure I don't have another stillborn child.

Once this child is born, I'll meet you at the jellyfish forest, and we can run away together. I think after this I would like to spend the rest of my days on a farm with you, far away from the glittering splendor of the castle.

Please stay safe until I can see you again.

Yours,
Aislin

That was the last letter Irsa ever received from Aislin.

Irsa didn't need to be at the memorial service to see that Aislin was dead; the tether that held them together snapped the moment it had happened. Still, she attended and watched from the shadows as Tynan and his seven daughters openly mourned Aislin. A soft sob left her. She believed Tynan had loved her in his way; it simply hadn't been enough to keep her alive.

The king turned to the gathering crowd, his daughter in

his arms. "Thank you for being here today to remember our queen. Our queen was a loving, warm, queen, and mother. Thank you for joining us to honor her today."

Irsa couldn't explain it, nor did she understand it, but his words filled her with fury. The way he spoke of Aislin as if she were merely an extension of himself and his kingdom lit a flame inside of Irsa, unlike any she'd experienced before. He hadn't even used her name for Amphitrite's sake! In a flash, she lost control of the low simmering rage, and she rushed forwards screaming. Her magic sprang forth, knocking over anyone in her way with glittering tentacles. Just before she reached Tynan and his daughters, a magical wall went up between them. Gavril stood between her and the king.

"Go home, Irsa," Gavril muttered smugly. "Before this gets worse."

"I don't have a home anymore!" She shrieked one tentacle of magic banging against the wall, causing it to crack. An arrow sped through the water, piercing her side. Blood pooled in the water, the magic scattering as she lost focus in her grief.

Someone had taken Tynan's children into the castle, and the king swam forward to meet Irsa, nose to nose. "From this day forth, Irsa of Tjena, you are hereby exiled from Alon," his words sparkled with his power, repeating 'exile' over and over on the tide. "Get out of my sight," he growled.

The words formed ropes, twining around her waist and dragging her through the city right to the very edge. There they dissipated. She swam forward, intent on returning to get her things, but they grabbed her again, yanking her back. '*Exile*,' they whispered on the tide.

"Have it your way, Tynan," Irsa growled. "I told you, I'd come back for her one day, and I will, you wait and see."

Irsa retreated to the darkness of the jellyfish forest. There, she allowed the grief and rage inside of her to fester and twist her magic. She let it grow more potent in her hate of the king. For years to come, she arose every morning, cursing his name, and vowing to avenge her darling Aislin.

Acknowledgments

First off, thank you—the reader—for reading Irsa's origin. I hope you enjoyed learning more about my version of the sea witch, and how she cam to be.

This story might be over, but this is not the last you have heard of Irsa. I hope to share more about her journey to finding happiness for herself soon.

Next, I'd like the think my small hoard of beta-readers. You guys gave some excellent insight, and I really appreciate the quick turn around that made this release possible!

And last but certainly not least, thank you to my small writing support group. Tiss, Elle, and Jasmine—without you there would be no Lou.

About the Author

Born and raised in a small town near the Chesapeake Bay, Lou Wilham grew up on a steady diet of fiction, arts and crafts, and Old Bay. After years of absorbing everything, there was to absorb of fiction, fantasy, and sci-fi she's left with a serious writing/drawing habit that just won't quit. These days, she spends much of her time writing, drawing, and chasing a very short Basset Hound named Sherlock.

When not, daydreaming up new characters to write and draw she can be found crocheting, making cute bookmarks, and binge-watching whatever happens to catch her eye.

Learn more about Lou and her future projects on her website: http://louinprogress.net or join her mailing list at: http://subscribepage.com/mailermailer

facebook.com/LouWilham

twitter.com/LouWilham

instagram.com/lou.wilham

Credits

Seaweed Free Icon made by smalllikeart from
www.flaticon.com/authors/smalllikeart

CPSIA information can be obtained
at www.ICGtesting.com
Printed in the USA
LVHW111818040220
645814LV00007B/1174